QUEEN OF THE ~~SIXTH~~

"You can't boss m— ...~~her~~ voice sounded so cool. ~~...~~ me to do." She left Ver~~onica~~ ...~~mouth~~ open and walked out of the cafeteria. It was totally against school rules to leave the cafeteria without a pass, but Robin didn't care. She had just broken the biggest rule of all by talking back to Veronica. Nothing the principal could do to her would be worse than Veronica's revenge.

"Robin is a likable, three-dimensional character; kids will enjoy making her acquaintance."

—*Kirkus Reviews*

QUEEN
—— OF THE ——
SIXTH GRADE

The Kids From

KENNEDY MIDDLE SCHOOL

QUEEN

OF THE

SIXTH GRADE

ILENE COOPER

Published by The Trumpet Club
a division of Bantam Doubleday Dell Publishing Group, Inc.
666 Fifth Avenue, New York, New York 10103

ISBN: 0-440-84291-3

This edition published by arrangement with Viking Penguin,
a division of Penguin Books USA Inc.
Printed in the United States of America
September 1990

10 9 8 7 6 5 4 3 2 1
OPM

For Harvey—the best

C H A P T E R
ONE

Robin Miller and the rest of the girls in Mrs. Volini's sixth grade class were in the locker room, waiting for Coach Brown to open the door to the gym. It was only the second day of school and confusion reigned.

The chalk hadn't arrived and Mrs. Volini had spent yesterday slamming through drawers and cupboards, looking for a piece that might have escaped the janitor during summer cleanup. The cafeteria workers cooked plenty of hot dogs for lunch, but there were no buns, so lonely pink weiners sat on plates next to tired pieces of white bread. Now Coach Brown couldn't find the keys to the gym.

The locker room was as stuffy as a closet, but no one except Robin seemed to mind. The

ica Volner and from her vantage point in the corner, Robin could see the effect Veronica was having on them as she shared her news.

"I haven't decided who's going to be in the AKGs yet," Veronica was saying in a bored voice, "but I really don't think a club should have more than six or seven members to start."

"What does AKG stand for?" someone demanded eagerly.

Veronica smiled a secret smile. "Only members can know that."

"When are you going to ask people to join?" Lisa Weissmann asked, looking confident that she'd be one of the chosen few.

"Maybe tomorrow." Veronica flipped her straight dark hair over one shoulder. "Curly and I are going to make invitations this afternoon."

Robin winced. She didn't like it when Veronica called her Curly, even though her mop of red curls made it a logical nickname. Who wanted a name that belonged to one of the Three Stooges? But Veronica thought it was cute, so Robin pretended she liked it, too.

Amanda Baxter spoke up, loud enough to be heard over the chattering girls. "If I don't get in, I might start my own club."

Robin shook her head. Silly Amanda. She

was always trying to pretend she was in Veronica's league, but she missed by a mile. No matter how hard she tried, and she tried hard, Amanda never got the hang of what the really cool girls at Kennedy Middle School were into. Like her discount store clothes, Amanda Baxter was just an imitation of the real thing.

"Really, a club of your own?" Veronica responded, amused.

"Yes, and I'm calling it the NFRs." Amanda looked around to see if she was getting any attention.

"NFRs? Let's see," Veronica said thoughtfully. "The Nerds for Real?"

Howls broke out and the words *Nerds for Real* were on everyone's lips.

"I suppose anyone who wants to be a nerd—for real—could join, but they might wait and see if they got into the AKGs first."

Luckily for Amanda, a perspiring Coach Brown hurried in with the key and opened the gym door, allowing her to slink in. Veronica lagged behind and pulled Robin's arm. "I think we're off to a good start," she whispered.

They were still laughing about Amanda's plans later that afternoon, sitting in Robin's backyard. Veronica reclined on the tattered excuse for a lounge chair while Robin sat cross-legged on the grass.

"When are you going to tell *me* what AKG stands for?" she asked, after the giggles died down.

"Oh, I don't know," Veronica replied without much interest.

"You said you would. Besides, how can I draw the invitations without knowing?" Robin tried very hard to keep a pleading note out of her voice.

"I don't want to give away too many club secrets."

Robin plucked a few blades of grass from the lawn and pretended great interest in wrapping them around her fingers.

"All right," Veronica decided. She leaned over conspiratorially, even though no one was around to hear. "Awesome Kennedy Girls," she whispered.

"Awesome Kennedy Girls," Robin repeated, her eyes shining. "That's great, Veronica!"

"I thought so, too," Veronica agreed without any false modesty.

"So who else is going to be in it?"

"Well, that's what I'm ready to decide. Get me some paper and a pencil and I'll make a list."

Robin obediently rose and hurried over to the porch, where she had thrown her backpack. Besides a pad and pen, she brought back a book to read. Knowing Veronica and her lists, Robin figured this might take a while.

Robin had been fully engrossed in her mystery for some time when Veronica's voice registered. "Does Jessica wear a bra?"

Barely raising her eyes from the page, Robin replied, "I don't know. I never noticed."

"Well, we don't want her if she is so immature that she doesn't. . . . Robin Miller, are you listening to me?"

"Sure." Robin looked up guiltily. "You were talking about Jessica's underwear."

"Not exactly. I'm trying to decide whether Jessica should be in the AKGs."

"Veronica, aren't you worried that we'll get some flack about starting a club? From our parents, or even the school, I mean. Clubs don't usually start until high school."

Veronica flashed Robin The Look, that one she had been giving her since the third grade. There was just the hint of a raised eyebrow and a secret smile. Some people wouldn't even notice The Look, but to Robin it was like a flash of lightning coming out of a clear sky. It said: "Trust me. I know exactly what I'm doing."

Veronica's confidence always seemed to rub off on Robin. "Of course, all the girls are crazy about the idea of a club," Robin continued more enthusiastically.

"I told you they would be. Tomorrow morning the future AKGs will get the good news."

"So who are they?" Robin prodded.

Veronica checked the piece of paper on which she had been scribbling and then read off each name importantly. "Kim Chapman, Natalie Wolk, Candy Dahl, Lisa Weissmann and Jessica Moriarity."

"If she wears a bra?"

"Right."

Robin absently fingered the straps of her undershirt, which were outlined against her yellow T-shirt. Veronica knew very well that she didn't wear a bra yet, but Robin guessed a flat chest was a concession she was willing to make for her best friend.

Veronica got off the lounge chair and stretched. "We're ready to make the invitations. Let's get started."

Robin scrambled off the grass and headed toward her back door. For the umpteen millionth time, she wished her house was more like Veronica's.

If Veronica had one of the larger homes in the neighborhood, Robin's had to be among the smallest. A squat brick ranch house, it had no discernible charm—one square room simply followed another. The cluttered kitchen led into a dining room just large enough to hold an oak table and chairs. Mrs. Miller called the set "antique." Robin called it "old."

Next came the living room lined with bookcases, all filled to overflowing. Robin's mother was a reference librarian at nearby Northwestern University and her father taught English at Forest Glen High School, so books came with the territory. Both of her parents thought lots of books made a room cozy, but considering the size of the living room, Robin felt it was cozy enough without bookshelves taking up most of the space.

On the shelves, books were crammed together in no particular order: fat textbooks sat next to Robin's battered *Mother Goose;* the Bible leaned against *Where the Wild Things Are.* There were even a few comic books stuffed into crevices, relics from Mr. Miller's boyhood. To Robin's acute embarrassment, her father still read them. Every once in a while, she'd come home to find him sprawled out on the chintz sofa, poring over *Scrooge McDuck.* Robin just shook her head when he said it relaxed him to read about Scrooge's money problems instead of his own.

Whatever Veronica thought about the Miller house, and she never said, there was one room where she always lingered—the kitchen. For the life of her, Robin couldn't figure out why Veronica liked it. The polka-dot curtains were faded and the Millers didn't even have a dishwasher. Still, it was the room Veronica seemed to like best.

Without waiting for an invitation, Veronica walked over to the chipped teddy bear cookie jar next to the stove and stuck her hand in. "Oh great. Chocolate chip," she said, pulling out an oversize cookie. "I was afraid your mother wouldn't bake because it's so hot."

Robin took a cookie, too. "My mother wouldn't let a few ninety-degree days stop her from baking." Or eating, she added silently. Her mother said laughingly that she wore her hobby around her hips, but Robin didn't think it was all that funny. Skinny as a broom handle herself, she couldn't imagine what it felt like to have extra padding.

"You want some milk?" Robin asked, and when Veronica nodded yes, Robin poured two glasses. "Let's take this to my room."

"I can't believe your mom lets you eat in your room," Veronica commented as she followed Robin down the hall.

"Why not? She knows I'll clean up after myself."

Robin stepped inside her room, her safe haven. If she couldn't control the way the rest of the house looked, she could and did see that her room was exactly the way she wanted it. No "antiques" for her. Her parents had allowed Robin's wealthy grandmother to buy her a bedroom set for her tenth birthday, so Robin and Nonnie had gone shopping together, coming home with a gleaming white platform bed, a dresser, a small desk and a chair. Robin had pored over books of wallpaper patterns, at last picking out a crisp pink-and-white check that her father had cheerfully spent a Saturday putting up.

Most of her friends plastered their walls with posters of rock stars and lined their beds and shelves with stuffed animals, but Robin only kept one Angora cat on her pink bedspread. Clothes were hung up and papers were stacked neatly on her desk. Veronica said it was unnatural to be so neat, but Robin reveled in it.

"Here," Robin said, shoving one of the paper plates and napkins she had grabbed in the kitchen at Veronica. "No crumbs."

"I know," Veronica grumbled. "But a person can take things too far," she added darkly.

"Well, we all don't have maids to pick up after us like some people I could mention."

"Helen's a housekeeper," Veronica corrected, settling herself carefully on the bed.

The distinction was lost on Robin. Helen cooked and cleaned while Mrs. Volner kept busy with her important job in an advertising agency in downtown Chicago. Whenever her own mother got upset about too much housework, she always yelled, "I am *not* a maid!"

"Let's get started on the invitations," Veronica urged. "I've got a good idea."

Robin went to her desk and pulled out some paper and colored markers. "I thought you said you wanted me to design them."

"I know, but listen, this is great," Veronica said, taking a bite of her cookie. "Draw an ice cube and the initials AKG inside."

"An ice cube?"

"Yes," Veronica replied impatiently, "because we're so cool."

It wasn't worth fighting about. Besides, the club was Veronica's idea, Robin reasoned, so if she wanted an ice cube, she might as well have one.

Robin sat down and began drawing with her blue pen. She added a few drops of water at the bottom so no one would think the ice cube was just a square. Then, in her best calligraphy, she wrote *AKG* in the center. Tentatively, she held it up for Veronica to see.

A smile lit Veronica's face. It couldn't really be called a pretty face. Her nose was too long and her eyes were just an ordinary brown. *Sophisticated* was a better word for her looks, partly because of her expression, which was usually bored, even petulant. But sometimes, mostly when she and Robin were alone, Veronica looked very peaceful.

"It's great," she told Robin. "I really like the way you did the lettering." She took the paper for a closer look. "Elegant," she praised.

Robin warmed with pleasure. "Thanks."

"Do you have any colored paper?"

"I think my mom does. Let me ask her." Robin hurried out to the sun porch, where she knew she'd find her mother working on the library budget, a task she loathed. But when Robin came into the cheery, book-filled room that doubled as her parents' office, Mrs. Miller was just sitting, staring out the picture window.

"Mom, I thought you were working."

Mrs. Miller turned and smiled. "Let's say I'm pre-working."

Robin giggled. "That's what I'll say the next time you ask me if I've done my homework."

Mrs. Miller pushed a wisp of her fading reddish hair over her ear. "Just try it," she said with mock ferocity. "Why don't you come over here and give your soon-to-be overworked mother a kiss?"

Robin grudgingly walked to her mother's desk chair. She was way too old to be kissed by her mother every hour of the day. But whenever she tried to explain that, Mrs. Miller always got a hurt look in her eyes that made Robin feel like a worm. It was easier to just submit.

"Mom," Robin said insistently as she wiggled out of the embrace, "I need to borrow some construction paper."

"What for?"

"Veronica and I are making something." A sixth sense told her that her mother might not like the idea of their forming an exclusive club. Mrs. Miller was very big on democracy. What she wasn't very big on was Veronica. Although Mrs. Miller was always nice to Veronica, she didn't like her. Robin really couldn't figure it out, though she had tried many times. Veronica was a good student, polite and, of course, popular. Why, she was practically queen of the sixth grade. As far as Robin was concerned, her mother should be thrilled that Veronica Volner wanted her daughter for a best friend.

"I guess I can spare some paper," Mrs. Miller said, reaching into the bottom drawer of her wooden desk.

Before her mother could think of any more questions, Robin thanked her and hurried away.

Stopping at the door of her bedroom, Robin was surprised to see Veronica standing at her dresser, studying a newly framed picture of Robin and her parents.

"What's so interesting about that?" Robin asked.

Veronica whirled around. "Nothing." She plunked the picture down on the dresser without another glance. "Did you get the paper?"

Robin held it out. "Uh-huh."

Grabbing several sheets, Veronica said, "Well, let's get started. And don't forget to leave a space for the time and date of the initiation."

"So when's it going to be?"

Veronica looked thoughtful. "My mother's going out of town next weekend. I could have a sleepover on Friday, just a week from tonight."

"I don't think my mom will let me sleep at your house if your mother's not there," Robin said doubtfully.

"Helen'll be home."

"Your mother will really let you have a sleepover for six girls while she's away?" Robin asked curiously.

Veronica's laugh was thin. "She'd prefer it. Besides, that's one reason we have a housekeeper—to do things my mother wants to avoid."

"I guess we can write up the invitations and switch it to my house if we have to."

Veronica considered this. "All right. But some of the things I have planned for the initiation would work better if Helen was in charge." Veronica looked at Robin significantly.

"What things?"

Veronica slid down on the floor next to Robin and said in a low voice, "Well, it'll all start when they arrive."

Robin listened, a squeal of delight escaping her lips every so often. Where did Veronica come up with these ideas, she wondered. Robin didn't care what her mother thought. Veronica was the most exciting best friend in the universe. There was nothing else Robin would rather be doing than sitting here, with Veronica whispering in her ear.

C H A P T E R
TWO

The next Friday Robin pushed her way onto the school bus and moved toward the back, where Candy Dahl, a soon-to-be AKG, was waving to her.

"Hey, here comes Robin Redbreast, looking for the Candy Doll!" Aaron Simon yelled before offering a loud burp.

"You're gross, Simple Simon," Robin said, deftly avoiding the foot Aaron had stuck out into the aisle. She eased into the hard seat Candy was saving. "Doesn't Aaron's mother ever drive him?" she complained.

"Hardly anyone gets driven to school except Veronica." Candy fluffed her blond wavy hair. With round blue eyes and a rosebud of a mouth, she did look something like a doll.

"Veronica's lucky her mother can drop her off on the way to work. She sure isn't missing anything by not riding this bus. Smells more like a gym than a bus anyway," Robin grumbled.

"I hope no one invites Aaron to the Halloween party," Candy said, making a face.

Despite Veronica's insistence that she wasn't going to divulge anything about the club until the formal initiation, she had been dropping nuggets of information all week. Her announcement of a Halloween party was one of them. There hadn't been a boy-girl party in the sixth grade yet and the news had spread fast.

"Aaron Simon? No way," Robin said firmly. There was only one boy Robin wanted to be there, but she wasn't about to discuss him with Candy.

Candy looked at Robin sideways. "You know what AKG stands for, don't you?"

Robin didn't try very hard to keep a note of pride out of her voice as she answered, "Yeah, I do."

"Can't you tell me?" And when Robin shook her head, Candy teased, "Just one little letter?"

Robin virtuously spouted Veronica's stock line: "You'll find out at the initiation." Then she added, "Only a few hours more."

"I can hardly wait," Candy said with a sigh.

Robin was relieved she was being allowed to go to Veronica's at all. Wisely, she hadn't mentioned the new club to her mother, and she withheld the information about the sleepover until a few other parents had given their consent. Then, to Robin's acute embarrassment, her mother had actually called the Volner house and talked to Helen. At last reassured, she had given Robin permission to attend.

For the rest of the ride, Candy chattered about who was in the club, who might get in and who was definitely out. Finally the bus came to a creaking halt in front of Kennedy Middle School.

Some of the kids said the red brick building resembled a prison, but Robin liked the school's strong sturdy look. It was originally built to house grades five through eight, but when the new upper school was completed, the seventh- and eighth-graders left Kennedy and the fourth-graders came in. As far as Robin was concerned, this was great. Most of the older kids were brats anyway, and the fourth-graders were easy to boss around. There were two sixth grade classes, Mrs. Volini's and Mr. Jacobs's, ready to rule the school. Robin figured, being a sixth-grader in Veronica's charmed circle was about as good as things gut. As she looked out the grimy bus window into the bustling schoolyard, her luck warmed her like a magic cloak.

Slowly, the kids began gathering their gear and moving off the bus. When she finally made her way to the open doors, Robin was hit with a wall of hot air. She didn't mind warm weather, but it was September and she'd appreciate a few leaves turning color at least. Instead, they hung green and sturdy on the trees, as though it was June.

"Come on," Robin called to Candy, who was lagging behind. "First bell." Mrs. Volini marked down for tardiness, so without stopping at her locker, she hurried toward her room. On the way in, she almost bumped into Gretchen Hubbard.

"Excuse me," Gretchen said softly.

"No problem," Robin muttered. Her eyes followed Gretchen as the girl sank into her seat. Gretchen was fat. She had thick blond braids and wide pale eyes. Her body resembled one of those dumplings Nonnie put into soup. These days Robin ignored Gretchen, but it hadn't always been that way.

Robin didn't let herself remember those other times very often, but today, while Mrs. Volini was busily taking attendance, Robin gazed into space and remembered when her best friend was not the fabulous Veronica Volner, but fat Gretchen Hubbard.

They had met the first day of kindergarten. Gretchen was standing outside the door of the classroom, bawling and clutching her mother's skirt. Robin had asked Mrs. Miller why the little girl was crying and received the answer: "Because she's afraid to leave her mother." Robin had marched over to Gretchen and said, "Don't cry. I'll take care of you." Wordlessly, Gretchen had taken Robin's hand and together they went into the kindergarten room. For the next three years, they were inseparable. Then, in the third grade, Veronica had come to Forest Glen and, after coolly looking over the crop of third-graders, she had chosen Robin to be her best friend.

Robin was never quite sure why she had been picked. Maybe it was because she had made Veronica laugh by whispering to her that their music teacher, a tall woman with wild curly hair and a bulbous nose, should be called Mrs. Bozo instead of Mrs. D'Roso. It wasn't all that funny—baby stuff, really—but Veronica had giggled until Mrs. D'Roso shushed her. Within days Robin and Veronica were always together.

Gretchen, of course, fell by the wayside, as easily forgotten as last year's Christmas pres-

cuts. Everyone else seemed to forget her, too. Sometimes Robin was surprised to still see her in class. But every once in a while, like now, Robin would look at Gretchen and feel a pang for those two little girls—one with blond braids, the other with a mop of curls—who always held hands.

Resolutely, Robin turned her attention to her work, opening her math book as Mrs. Volini instructed. With no air-conditioning, the room was stifling and more than once Robin felt her eyes grow heavy. Then Mrs. Volini said something that made her snap to attention.

"I'm ready to choose reading partners today."

Robin and Veronica, who sat across the room, exchanged looks. They had already decided to be partners.

"As you know, the reading partners will each read the same book, and give a joint oral report on it. I'd like to see some lively conversation about what made the book good or bad. Now, as far as choosing partners, I don't want you pairing up with your friends. So I have decided to pick partners for you."

A huge groan went up from the class.

Mrs. Volini ran a hand through her short brown hair. "I am doing this entirely fairly," she admonished them. "All of your names have been put into a paper bag. Since we have an even number, it should work out perfectly."

Perfectly for you, Robin thought to herself.

In her precise manner, Mrs. Volini began picking names out of the bag, two by two. When Robin heard Veronica's name, she sat up straight, hoping that fate might have thrown the two of them together; then she heard Candy called as Veronica's partner. Great. Who was she going to be stuck with now, Robin wondered.

"Robin Miller and Jonathan Rossi."

Robin could feel a blush as red as her hair coming to her face. She quickly lowered her head and pretended great interest in the cover of her history book. Jonathan! Jonathan was the nicest, best-looking boy in the class. Robin had a crush on him that was so powerful—so secret—she had never even told Veronica about it.

Later, at lunchtime, when Robin was bringing her empty tray to the conveyor belt, Jonathan came up to her. She had known Jonathan almost all her life—they had even gone to nursery school together. But this summer when she saw him playing basketball in the park, her heart had suddenly done a little flip-flop. She had wondered why she'd never noticed what friendly brown eyes he had. And the way he carelessly kept pushing his brown hair off his forehead. After that she had taken special trips to the park, just to watch him play basketball, bringing along bread crumbs so she could pretend she was feeding the squirrels.

It was hard keeping a secret from Veronica, but her fear that Veronica might tease her about having a crush was enough to close Robin's lips. As for Jonathan, he was nice to her, just as he had been when they were five, and eight and ten, but he never paid any *special* attention to her. Now they were going to have to spend time together as reading partners. Her heart did its familiar little spin.

"Hey, Miller, what book do you want to do for our report?" he asked, taking a final sip of his milk before throwing the container on the moving belt.

He looked so adorable with a milk mustache! Robin gave what she hoped was a casual shrug. "Have you read *The Wolves of Willoughby Chase?*"

"No. Have you read *The Baseball Life of Darryl Strawberry?*"

"There's a baseball player named Strawberry?" Robin giggled.

"Hey, being named for a fruit is no funnier than being named for a bird, Robin." He gave her a friendly punch in the arm.

Robin wanted to caress the spot where he

touched her. Instead, she pretended indifference. "We'd better go to the library and find something we both want to read." She held her breath—had she gone too far? But Jonathan didn't seem to notice anything unusual in the request. "Sure," he said. "Maybe Sunday. I'll call you."

With that he loped away to join some of the other boys heading out to the schoolyard. "Sunday," Robin whispered.

"Are you talking to yourself?" Veronica's strident voice broke into her thoughts.

Robin bit her lip guiltily. "No, of course not."

"I hope not." Veronica placed her tray on the conveyor belt. "They put people in the loony bin for that. So what did Jonathan want?" she asked casually.

"Oh, we were just talking about being reading partners," Robin said, deliberately keeping her answer vague.

"You know, it's really lucky that you wound up with him as a partner."

Robin gave Veronica a sharp look. "Lucky? Why?"

Veronica smiled noncommittally. "You'll see. It fits into my plans."

Robin worried for the rest of the afternoon. What kind of plans could Veronica possibly have for Jonathan?

CHAPTER

THREE

Veronica's cryptic comment about Jonathan nagged at Robin and, although she tried to think of a way to bring up his name casually so she could find out what Veronica meant, nothing came to mind.

Jonathan got pushed to the background anyway, with all the preparations for the initiation that took place after school. There always seemed to be one more thing Veronica wanted to do.

"Boy," Robin grumbled that afternoon as she set up the folding chairs, "if I had had any idea how much work this thing was going to be, I would have . . ."

Veronica stood on a stepladder, her voice muffled by the black cotton material she was taping over the rec room windows. "What?"

What would she have done? Robin thought. Not participated? Hardly. "I guess I would have told you to tone things down a little," she finally muttered.

Veronica jumped off the stepladder. "No way. My brother told me that the initiation ceremony at his fraternity is a really big deal and ours is going to be, too."

Robin looked around the room, which was dark even when the windows weren't covered. Tonight it would really look creepy. They had even hung a few paper skeletons and bats on the wall, which frugal Robin had reminded Veronica could be used for decorations at the Halloween party. "Everything looks ready."

"Did you check the refrigerator?"

"Yeah, but Helen wasn't too happy about all the stuff in there."

Veronica giggled. "Helen thinks we're going to be performing a Black Mass or something."

"I know. What about when you told her to stay in her room and not come down, even if she heard screams?"

Veronica imitated Helen's quavery voice. " 'Screams! You never said anything about screams.' "

Both Robin and Veronica burst out laughing. After she caught her breath, Robin asked, "Do you think she'll tell your mother?"

Veronica shrugged. "My mother knows it's a

club initiation. I'm sure she expects things to get a little wild."

"Really?" Robin asked enviously. "My mother always wants things to be quiet."

"Well, your mother's nice in other ways." Veronica changed the subject abruptly. "I've got to get downtown before the shops close."

"I'll go with you," Robin offered. "We can ride our bikes."

"Uh-uh. I have to go alone."

"More club secrets?" At Veronica's nod, Robin threw up her hands. "Don't say it, I know. I'll find out tonight."

Veronica put her arm around Robin's shoulders. "Come back early, before the others get here. After all, you're practically the AKG cofounder."

"I am?" Robin said, enormously flattered.

"You helped a lot," Veronica praised. "Besides," she added practically, "you're the only one who knows how the initiation's going to work. You've got to help me keep things moving."

Robin tried to get to Veronica's early, but after dinner her mother insisted she talk long-distance to Nonnie. By the time she huffed and puffed up Veronica's front stairs, it was almost seven.

"Is anyone here yet?" she asked as soon as

Veronica let her in.

"Nope, but it won't be long." Veronica, looking great in a hand-painted T-shirt and jeans, was as excited as Robin had ever seen her.

She followed Veronica into her elegant living room and settled herself uncomfortably on the peach silk sofa. Veronica's house was like something out of a magazine, beautiful and pristine, as though no one actually lived there. Although Robin envied Veronica her surroundings, she had to admit she liked looking at the rooms more than she enjoyed spending time in them.

Veronica was peering out the window. "Here come Candy and Jessica," she said eagerly. At the first ring of the doorbell, she composed herself and then opened the door. "Welcome, future AKGs."

Jessica, a short girl with a pixie haircut, gave a nervous laugh, but Veronica cut her off in mid-giggle. "This is a solemn occasion," she informed Jessica sternly. "Put your sleeping bags and stuff over in the corner and sit down. No talking until the others arrive."

Candy and Jessica dutifully took a seat on the matching couch across from Robin. Even though Robin knew what awaited the other girls in the basement, she felt almost as nervous as they looked.

The doorbell rang shrilly again, and Lisa Weissmann came in dressed in shorts and a T-shirt, her wheat-colored hair in French braids. "Boy, it's still hot out there." She chattered on until she noticed no one was responding. "What's wrong?" she demanded.

Candy and Jessica just looked at her, afraid to answer. Robin decided to let Veronica do the talking.

"Nothing's wrong," Veronica replied. "Just take a seat until we're ready to start."

An unnatural silence hung over the room. Robin looked over at Candy, who was fidgeting on the couch, and Jessica staring off into space. Lisa, who normally couldn't go five minutes without talking, was biting her fingernail, as though keeping something in her mouth would keep the words from popping out.

Veronica began pacing on the plush gray carpeting. "I told everyone to be here by seven." Frowning at the ornate mantel clock, she noted, "It's almost a quarter after now. People can be uninvited to be AKGs, you know," she added ominously.

A few moments later there was a knock at the door. "It's about time," Veronica muttered.

"You're late," she said shortly, ushering in

Kim and Natalie. Robin always thought it was funny that Kim and Natalie looked so much alike, even though Kim was half-Chinese. They both had sparkling brown eyes and shiny dark hair that hung straight to their chins. Best friends, they played in the band and were fearless when it came to sports. It might be easy to frighten Candy, or shy little Jessica, but Robin had a suspicion that Kim and Natalie were a lot tougher.

"So," Veronica said, coming to the center of the room. "We're all here. At last." She looked pointedly at Kim and Natalie.

Kim tried to explain their tardiness. "My mother . . ." she began, but Veronica shot her a withering look and her words faded away.

"Now," Veronica resumed, "I will lead the way to the Hall of Initiation. Robin will be behind you. Follow me," she commanded.

As the group went through the kitchen, Kim laughingly said, "Is this the Hall of Initiation, or the basement?"

Veronica stopped dead in her tracks and turned to face the offending Kim. "For your information, it's a rec room, not a basement, and if you're going to joke around . . ."

"I'm not," Kim said, trying to wipe the smile from her face.

"All right then," Veronica snapped. She

grabbed a flashlight from the kitchen counter, turned it on and started down the rec room stairs.

From her vantage point at the rear of the line, Robin could see Jessica nervously twisting the bottom of her blouse while the darkness of the stairwell made Natalie reach behind her for Kim's hand. When the girls had finally stumbled downstairs, Veronica assembled them into a circle. The only light came from the few flashlights Veronica had set up strategically in corners.

"You've been invited here to join the AKGs, but there are several tests you're going to have to pass. Robin, offer them the hand of friendship."

Robin's eyes had adjusted to the dark enough for her to make her way to the table they had carefully arranged that afternoon. She picked up a cold clammy object.

"Ugh!" Jessica screamed shrilly as she touched it.

Robin shoved it at Lisa. "What is it?" Lisa yelled, almost dropping the "hand."

As Robin suspected, Kim wasn't so easily fooled. "It's just a rubber glove filled with ice or something," she said. And Natalie, who believed Kim, shook it without a word. But Candy didn't seem to hear her. "It's like a dead person's hand," she said, shivering.

"Now, come over and eat some worms," Veronica intoned.

Even Robin, who had helped boil the spaghetti to be used as the worms, had to admit her throat closed a little as she swallowed the strands soaked with cooking oil. They just tasted so slimy. It was disgusting, too, to stick her hand in a bowl of peeled grapes, doubling as eyeballs.

Most of the girls alternated between nervous laughter and shrieks, but Jessica was almost crying. Even in the dim shadows Robin could see Veronica frowning at her. Jessica had better watch it, Robin thought to herself. Crybabies hardly fit in with the sophisticated image Veronica wanted for the AKGs.

"You've all passed the first stage of the entry on the road to becoming AKGs. More or less." Veronica glared at Jessica, who was clutching a piece of tissue in her hand. Then she nodded at Robin, who took the hand, the worms and the eyeballs behind the bar.

"Now, I'm going to read the AKG rules. Listen carefully and see if you're willing to abide by them." Veronica motioned to the girls to sit in the circle of chairs and picked up a legal pad off the table and began reading. "One. I will obey the club rules."

"But what are the club rules?" Natalie interrupted.

"I'm about to tell you. And hold all your questions to the end," Veronica added, sounding exactly like Mrs. Volini. "Two. I will be loyal to my club sisters. Three. No secrets of the club will be divulged. Four. The first president of the club will be the founder, Veronica Volner. Now, does anyone want to ask anything?"

There was silence, so Veronica said, "All right then, is everyone willing to take the oath of allegiance?"

The girls looked at each other excitedly. "Yes," Kim answered for all of them.

"Good," Veronica said with a small smile. "Raise your right hands and repeat after me. I swear to be a loyal and dedicated member of the AKGs."

It sounded a little garbled, but all the prospective members said the pledge.

"Do you swear to uphold the club rules?"

The six girls said as one, "I swear."

"Congratulations. You are all official Awesome Kennedy Girls."

Excited murmurs went around the circle. "Awesome." "Great name." "Everyone's going to go nuts, guessing," Kim added.

"Well, you can't tell them," Veronica said

flatly. "That's one of the club secrets that you just swore never to tell."

"Veronica's right," Candy agreed. "And maybe we should start dressing alike or something. You know, like some kind of a club sign."

"I've already thought of that," Veronica said, going behind the bar. She came out with a shopping bag and handed out little white boxes topped with gold bows, one to each girl. There were squeals as the members opened them up and found square gold pins engraved with the initials *AKG*.

"Are they real gold?" Lisa asked as she pinned hers onto her T-shirt.

Veronica hesitated. "They're gold-filled. I didn't want to get gold in case someone lost hers."

Robin fingered the small pin with its fancy lettering. So that's why Veronica had to get to town this afternoon. Despite Veronica's explanation, Robin figured Veronica couldn't afford real gold, but these were just as nice. Even gold-filled pins must have cost a bundle, Robin knew, and she suspected that Veronica had gotten the money from her father.

Ever since the Volners' divorce, Mr. Volner couldn't do enough for Veronica—except make time to see her. He lived downtown in a Chicago high rise overlooking Lake Michigan and always complained it was such a long ride out to Forest Glen, although when he lived at home he commuted back and forth every day just like a lot of mothers and fathers. Veronica pretended she didn't care about seeing her father. She sarcastically called him "Chicago's hope for single women," or demanded lavish presents, which she always got, but Robin remembered before the divorce when Veronica tagged everywhere after her dad. She loved him a lot then.

With the initiation over, the AKGs made themselves comfortable on the couch and the floor and began hashing out plans for the club.

"The other girls are going to ask if we're going to take in new members. Are we?" Lisa wondered.

"Well, we have all the really good ones right now," Kim said, grabbing a handful of potato chips from the bowl Veronica had set out.

"Leave the rest of them for Amanda's Nerds For Real," Natalie said to laughter.

"No new members for a while," Veronica decreed. "Why don't we order the pizza now? I'm hungry."

While waiting for the pizza, the AKGs voted on club officers and set the amount of club dues. Then the party began in earnest.

Veronica put on some tapes and Candy brought out the makeup tray she had swiped from her older sister. It contained twelve eye shadows, five lipsticks, four blushers, three nail polish bottles, two eye pencils and a mascara.

"Make me up, Natalie," Kim demanded. "Let's practice for the Halloween party."

Lisa was unbraiding her hair. "Who are you going to invite?" she asked Kim.

"Gee, I don't know," Kim replied, rubbing a lipstick on her hand and critically looking at the color. "What about you?"

"Maybe Bobby Glickman. He's practically famous, after all."

Natalie snorted. "I don't think being in one fried chicken commercial makes him famous."

"He's going to be in another one," Candy interjected, holding up a hand mirror and carefully outlining her cupid bow mouth.

Lisa looked put out that she didn't know the news about Bobby first. "Where did you hear that?"

"His mother told my mother," Candy replied. "Corn flakes."

"Pardon me?" Lisa said, confused.

"That's what the commercial's for. Corn flakes."

"Oh. What about you, Jessica?" Lisa asked, turning toward Jessica, who was sitting quietly in the corner. "Who are you going to ask to the party?"

"I thought I might invite Jonathan."

Robin and Veronica both snapped to attention at this, but it was Veronica who spoke. "Jessica," she started slowly, "I don't think you want to ask Jonathan."

"I don't?" Jessica said blankly.

"No. Because I might invite him myself."

Now it was Robin's turn to stare at Veronica. When had she decided that?

With her huge eyes and tiny body, Jessica looked more like a little kid than ever. "Maybe . . . Maybe I'll try someone else."

"Good idea." Veronica beamed as though she was a teacher whose slowest student had just given the right answer.

The fun had gone out of the evening for Robin. She tried to smile while Lisa put eye makeup on her, she even swallowed a few bites of pizza, but they didn't go down past the knot in her stomach. She was dying to get Veronica alone and at the same time dreading their conversation.

Finally, much later, after the makeup and pizza and dancing, Veronica and Robin pulled their sleeping bags together in the corner, but it was Veronica who raised the subject of Jonathan.

"Everybody had a great time, didn't they?" Veronica asked, punching her pillow.

"Yeah."

Before Robin could say more, Veronica continued, "And the Halloween party is going to be wonderful. I had to set Jessica straight about Jonathan, though. Not that he'd be interested in her. What a baby."

Robin huddled in her sleeping bag. "When did you decide you wanted to go with him?" she said softly.

"Well, he's the obvious choice. I mean, he's super good-looking, and the star of the basketball team, but most important, he's tall."

"Tall?"

"Yes," Veronica said, trying to find a comfortable spot on the floor. "Think about it. There aren't too many sixth grade boys that are as tall as I am. Oh, there's Artie, but he's a geek, and I can't stand Jamie Bowen. That leaves Jonathan."

Robin was disgusted. Veronica wanted Jonathan because of his height! She didn't even care how nice he was.

Oblivious to Robin's feelings, Veronica rattled on, "And this whole thing with you being Jon's reading partner is working out great.

Now you can spend time talking to Jonathan about me. You can find out if he'll go with me to the party."

"Can't you find out yourself?" Robin asked, trying to keep the irritation out of her voice.

Veronica frowned. "No. My mother says you never put yourself on the line. I have to make sure he wants to be my boyfriend."

Boyfriend! This was getting worse and worse, Robin thought. She stared silently at the ceiling.

"Why are you being so weird about this? You don't like him yourself, do you?"

"Of course not," a startled Robin lied. Why tell the truth now that Veronica had staked her claim?

"Then what's your problem?" When Robin didn't answer, Veronica said in a silky voice, "I really need you, Curly. You could be like the little boy in *The Go-Between*. Did you ever see that movie?"

Robin shook her head.

"Well, probably not. It was a foreign film. I saw it on cable. Anyway, it's about these lovers and this kid goes back and forth between them, delivering messages."

"I'm not a little boy and you're not lovers." Robin rolled away from Veronica.

"Come on, Robin," Veronica said persuasively. "I'm just saying you could do me a big favor by talking to Jonathan and paving the way. It would mean a lot." She put her hand on Robin's shoulder. "He's perfect for me."

Robin stared at the paneled wall. What choice did she have? Even without her help, Veronica would find a way to let Jonathan know how she felt, and once he knew, he'd never bother with Robin anyway. Why, he'd probably be mad at her for not bringing them together sooner. Veronica and Jonathan both angry at her, she thought glumly. She could see it all now. With a sigh, Robin turned back toward Veronica. "I'll do what I can," she said flatly.

Even in the darkness, Robin could see Veronica's smile. "Terrific. I knew I could count on you."

C H A P T E R
FOUR

Robin had to give her mother credit. She was nothing if not observant. Eating her lunch at the kitchen table the next day, Robin was startled when Mrs. Miller asked her, "What's that on your pocket?"

The small gold pin blended so well with the plaid of her shirt that Robin had been sure it was practically invisible. Still crabby from her news of last night, Robin didn't feel like getting into a hassle. But when she glanced across the table at her mother, she could see Mrs. Miller was definitely waiting for an answer.

"It's my club pin," Robin answered after a few seconds.

Mrs. Miller frowned. "And what club is that?"

Robin knew that if she responded, "AKG," those mysterious initials would open up a whole new line of questioning. "Just a club we decided to start last night at Veronica's." She tried to be nonchalant as she took a bite of her turkey sandwich.

"If you formed the club last night, how did you get pins already?" Mrs. Miller grilled her.

Robin had to think fast. This was getting complicated. "Veronica got them as a surprise."

"Oh, Veronica did."

Just the way her mother said Veronica's name grated on Robin. Whatever problems she was having with Veronica, Mrs. Miller's tone made Robin want to spring to her defense. "Everybody loved the pins."

Mrs. Miller played with her napkin. "May I know who's in this club?"

"Jessica, Lisa, Candy, Kim and Natalie." Robin said their names with satisfaction. Mrs. Miller knew all those girls and most of their mothers, too.

"Hmmm" was her only response.

Robin decided to press her advantage. "You're always telling me I should have more friends, so now I have a whole club full of them."

Mrs. Miller got up, refilled the kettle and

put it on the stove. "Does this club have a name?"

Darn, Robin thought. She should have known she couldn't get away from this line of questioning for long. "It's called the AKGs and I can't tell you what the initials mean," she replied in a rush.

"And why not?" her mother inquired, turning to face Robin.

"Because it's a secret," Robin said defiantly.

Mrs. Miller sighed. "I'm not sure I like the idea of a secret club, Robin."

Robin wanted to say, "Well, I don't care," but she was afraid to. "Nobody can tell," she finally muttered.

"Nobody can tell what?" Mr. Miller came into the kitchen, sweaty from mowing the grass. He repeated his question as he washed up at the sink. "Nobody can tell what?"

The tea kettle whistled and Mrs. Miller refilled her blue ceramic cup. "Your daughter belongs to some sort of a secret club."

Mr. Miller came over and ruffled Robin's hair as he sat down. "So?"

Robin immediately brightened, while Mrs. Miller rolled her eyes. "Oh, Jack, you don't mean that."

"Sure I do." He grabbed some turkey and rye bread off the platter and began fixing himself a sandwich. "Kids have secret clubs all the time."

Robin didn't say anything, but she shot her mother a triumphant look.

"I don't know what needs to be so hush-hush," Mrs. Miller murmured as she sat down.

"Being a kid is all about keeping secrets. Don't you remember that, Lois?" Mr. Miller winked at Robin, who tried to suppress a smile.

"Do you know the other girls in the club?" Mr. Miller continued.

"Yes," Robin's mother answered reluctantly.

"Nice kids?"

"Most of them," she said in a careful voice.

Mr. Miller poured a glass of milk. "Then what's the harm?" He turned to Robin. "You're not a gang, are you? Not planning to pull off any robberies? Fight other gangs with switchblade knives?"

"Nope," Robin said cheerfully. "But we do want to have a boy-girl Halloween party." Her dad was in such a good mood, it seemed a good idea to fight this battle now.

Her parents exchanged a look. Then her father said slowly, "Boy-girl party, huh?"

Surprisingly, it was her mother who seemed to understand. "I knew it had to happen eventually," she said. "I went to my first boy-girl party when I was in the sixth grade."

"You did?" Robin couldn't conceal her surprise.

Even Mrs. Miller had to laugh. "Yes, do you think Nonnie locked me up in a tower until I was twenty-one?"

"No, but I didn't know that back then . . ."

Her father groaned. "Please not with the 'back then.' We weren't exactly riding around on dinosaurs."

"We even had rock 'n' roll," Mrs. Miller informed Robin. "I happen to remember that first party very well. My friend Dale and I both liked Stevie Kaye, and this Elvis Presley record was playing, so he danced with the two of us at the same time. It was a Valentine's Day party and we each fed him candy hearts," Mrs. Miller recalled dreamily.

Trust her mother to work out things so amicably, Robin thought with irritation. She could almost see herself sharing a dance with Veronica and Jonathan.

The phone rang and Robin jumped up. "I'll get it," she said, running into the living room, even though there was a phone hanging on the kitchen wall.

"Hello?" she said breathlessly.

"Robin, it's Jonathan."

Robin had been hoping that Jonathan would call about going to the library as he said he would. But actually hearing his voice made her nervous. "Hi, Jon," she replied softly.

For a moment there was an awkward silence, then Jonathan said, "Do you still want to go to the library tomorrow?"

"Sure." Robin wracked her brain for something else to say. "What time?"

"How about we get there when it opens, right at one?"

One. At that moment, it was the most wonderful number in the world! "Uh, one would be fine," she said, making an effort to keep her voice level.

"Okay, see you then," Jonathan said cheerfully. " 'Bye."

" 'Bye." Robin hung up the receiver, but kept her hand on it for a few seconds. She knew there was no reason to get excited. They were just meeting about an assignment. And topic B was going to be Veronica. Somehow it didn't matter. She was spending the afternoon with Jonathan Rossi.

Robin got up early on Sunday and began rifling through her closet, looking for something to wear, but nothing she owned seemed nice enough for this momentous occasion. Robin glanced in the mirror, holding up a pink blouse to herself. She wrinkled her nose. Why hadn't she ever noticed how badly pink went with her red hair? With disgust, she flung the blouse into a corner.

Finally Robin put on a denim work shirt and her best jeans. It wasn't much, but it was the best she could do. At least Jonathan wouldn't guess how excited she was by this meeting— not by the way she was dressed, anyway.

Robin still had hours before she had to leave, so she went down to the empty kitchen and fixed herself some cereal and a glass of juice.

Carrying her food out to the rickety table on the back porch, she carefully put it down and pulled up one of the wooden patio chairs. As she dipped into her cereal, Robin thought about Veronica's request that Robin be her go-between.

Veronica, of course, didn't know that Robin liked Jonathan, too, but Robin suspected it wouldn't have made a difference if she did. What other people wanted wasn't of much interest to Veronica.

Robin's eye caught sight of a cardinal flying by, a streak of red against the green leaves. That's the way Veronica was, bright and exciting. Robin took another bite of her cereal, then pushed it away. It was as dry as sand.

Mr. Miller came out of the house, yawning, his black hair sticking up in every direction. "You're up awfully early."

Robin looked at her watch. "It's almost

eleven o'clock, Daddy. You're up late."

He sat down beside her. "I guess so. Say, why don't we fix your mother some breakfast in bed?"

"Do I have to?" The words slipped out.

"Sugar, what's with you and your mom? You used to be so close."

Robin dipped her spoon in and out of her mushy cereal. "I don't know," she said quietly. "We just don't get along that well."

"Yes, but why?"

Robin looked up into her father's green eyes, so like her own. "She doesn't like my friends, and she's always trying to tell me what to do."

Mr. Miller laughed, making Robin's temper flare.

"You ask me what's wrong and then you laugh at me!" She rose to leave, but her father grabbed her wrist and pushed her gently back down on the seat. "I'm sorry," he said, "but using their authority is what parents do, hon. It's part of the oath they make you take at the Parents' Training Academy."

Robin's lip twitched. "And you went to the Parents' Training Academy?"

"Oh absolutely. I graduated summa cum laude. I learned all the key phrases, like 'Pick up your clothes'; 'Where are you going, young lady?'; 'Don't use that tone of voice with me. . . .' "

"Mom learned all those phrases, too."

Mr. Miller turned serious. "Just remember, Robin, you're growing up and it's hard on her. She just wants to do what's best for you."

Robin stopped listening. She had heard it all before.

"So do you want to help me make breakfast?"

"I guess." Robin shrugged. She supposed it would make the time go by faster.

And it did help. By the time they finished making French toast and bacon and serving it to a delighted Mrs. Miller, it was time to bike to the library. When she arrived, it was already a little after one.

Robin wandered around the stacks for a few minutes until she came back into the magazine area of the reading room, where she spotted Jonathan over in a corner, leafing through *Sports Illustrated*.

"Hi," she said shyly, coming up behind him.

"Oh hi." He put the magazine down.

Robin ran a sweaty palm down the front of her jeans. "Ready to pick out a book?"

"Sure."

To her relief, Robin didn't have to worry about making conversation. Jonathan talked away, full of ideas for their project. "I think we should pick a book neither of us has read before," he said as they moved into the children's department.

"Good idea. That way we won't know if either of us liked it until we're done."

Jonathan stepped around a little kid who was reading a picture book on the red carpet. "What do you like to read about?"

Robin thought for a minute. "Stories with girls in them."

Jonathan grinned. "Well, we already have some controversy. I like to read books about boys. Do you like adventure stories?"

"I hate 'em," Robin said honestly. "What about mysteries?"

"They're all right, I guess." Jonathan looked around the shelves as though he had never paid much attention to them before. "Can't you find us something good? Your mother's a librarian, isn't she?"

"She works at the university, but sure, I can pick something." Robin felt a weight descending on her shoulders.

Glancing around the room for inspiration, she caught sight of a book displayed with a number of others on top of the case along the wall. Jonathan followed her as she plucked it down. *The Westing Game*," Robin said, handing it to him. "Kim read it and said it was great."

Jonathan opened the inside cover, where it told what the book was about. Smiling as he read, he finally looked up and said, "Neat. It sounds funny."

Vastly relieved at his approval, Robin told him, "You can check this one out. My mother will buy me a copy."

Jonathan flipped it up in the air and caught it behind his back.

Robin giggled. "This isn't a basketball court, Jon."

"I gotta keep in practice until the season starts, don't I?"

Robin walked slowly toward the vestibule, with Jonathan next to her, assessing the chances of the Kennedy Middle School basketball team. He continued talking as he checked out his book at the busy circulation desk. Robin almost panicked when she realized they were finally at the door and she hadn't even mentioned Veronica's name. Then Jonathan offered a reprieve. "Do you want to go over to The Hut and get some ice cream?"

"Sure," Robin responded, a little too quickly.

Jonathan grew red in the face. "I mean, if you have your own money."

"Of course I have my own money," Robin said, her own embarrassment keen. She had known what he meant when he mentioned ice cream. What did he think, she was some kind of a moron?

"Let's go then," Jonathan said, stepping into the bright sunlight and unlocking his bike.

They wheeled their bikes down picturesque Main Street to the very outskirts of town. There were other, fancier, ice cream parlors in Forest Glen, but all the kids from Kennedy and the upper school hung out at The Hut. Run-down, with worn wooden sides that were once painted red—it really was a hut. Some people insisted it was an eyesore that should be torn down, but the best hot dogs in town were served there, as well as four different flavors of ice cream that were made fresh every day.

After debating the merits of vanilla fudge versus cherry nut and making their choices, Robin and Jonathan wandered outside, where some rickety benches were set up on the small patch of grass behind The Hut.

Robin was relieved to see they were alone except for a man and his toddler son who had ice cream from his lips to his eyebrows. It was going to be hard enough to make conversation without other people around. The dad didn't count; he was too busy trying to wipe his son's face with a napkin to pay any attention to them.

Even though they had just been sitting

down for a few moments, the silence was already starting to seem very long to Robin. With a sigh, she decided it might be time to bring up Veronica. "You know," she began, "some of the girls just formed a new club."

"Yeah?" Jonathan seemed more interested in his ice cream than in a girls' club.

"It's called the AKGs. I can't tell you what it means." With no response, Robin plunged ahead. "Veronica's the president."

"That figures."

Robin was shocked. It almost sounded as if Jonathan didn't like Veronica. "What do you mean?"

"Well, she kind of runs the girls, doesn't she?"

"I guess so," Robin said, though she wasn't sure she cared for that characterization.

"So naturally, she'd be president." He pitched the remains of his cone into a nearby basket. "It's good!" he shouted like a sports announcer.

Robin was still nervously nibbling at her ice cream. "Veronica's very well organized. That's one reason she's president."

"Mmm," Jonathan replied, sounding bored.

"It was her idea to have a party. With boys."

Now Jonathan showed some interest. Leaning toward her, he asked, "When?"

This would be something to tell Veronica.

"Halloween. I . . . wasn't sure the boys would want to come," Robin said tentatively.

Jonathan smiled. "Sure. Why not?" When Robin didn't reply, he looked up at the clouds and said, "You're all right."

As she slowly pedaled home, Robin kept turning that phrase over in her mind. "You're all right," she murmured. Did that mean Jonathan thought she, personally, was all right, or that all the girls were?

Robin would have liked to hug the details of the afternoon close to herself for a while, but the phone was ringing as she walked in the door. She had barely said hello when Veronica broke in, "I called earlier. Your mother said you'd gone to the library with Jonathan. How did it go?"

Pulling the cord of the phone into the hall closet, Robin made herself comfortable on the tiny piece of floor space. "Fine. We spent most of the time talking about the report, of course . . ."

"What did he say about me?"

Robin had planned for this question. "He wasn't surprised you were president of AKGs."

"Why not?"

"Well, because of your leadership abilities." Robin thought this sounded infinitely better than the way Jonathan had phrased it.

"Really?"

53

Robin could almost see Veronica running her hand through her hair, the way she always did when she was pleased.

"And he's looking forward to the party."

"You already told him about the party?" Veronica squealed. "Terrific. What else did he say?"

"That's about all."

"You mean, he didn't say anything else about me?"

"He didn't say anything else about anything."

"Oh, Robin." A little pout had crept into her voice.

"I did the best I could," Robin replied defensively.

There were a few seconds of silence. "I suppose it's a start. Besides," Veronica brightened, "there will be other times you can get together and talk about me."

After Robin hung up, she sat alone in the dark closet and thought about Veronica's words. She told the coats and boots what she wished she could say to Veronica: "But I want to get together with Jonathan and talk about *me*."

C H A P T E R
FIVE

The AKGs had caused a sensation when the club was just an idea. But that was nothing compared to the excitement that exploded when they showed up on Monday in the schoolyard actually wearing their pins. Girls from both sixth grade classes ringed Veronica, Candy and Lisa, while Natalie and Kim were a short distance away at the playing field, showing off their pins to a couple of fifth-graders.

Robin overslept and had to be driven to school, much to her mother's disgust. She bounded out of the car with hardly a wave to Mrs. Miller and ran over to join Veronica's group. Lightly, Veronica flicked a piece of lint from the Michigan State sweatshirt her brother had sent her. "We might take new members," she was saying.

"Do we apply?" someone asked.

"No, we pick you."

"Then what do we have to do?" the same person wondered.

Veronica smiled. "Anything we say."

Noting Robin's presence, Veronica pulled her outside the circle, while Candy took off her pin and passed it around. "Gee, this is better than . . ." Robin started, but Veronica wasn't interested in discussing the impression the AKGs were making.

"I've been thinking. You missed a good opportunity yesterday, Robin. You should have found out how he feels about being my date."

Robin scuffed the toe of her gym shoe against the gravel. "I couldn't just blurt that out."

"You can't get too subtle, Curly. You know how stupid boys can be."

"Jonathan's not stupid," Robin said hotly.

A curious look crept into Veronica's eyes. "That's not what I meant. But like my mom says about her boyfriends, you have to lead them in the right direction."

Robin thought this made men sound like dogs, but she let it go. For someone who didn't see her mother all that much, Veronica sure liked to quote her.

"If you don't keep talking about me, he

might lose interest," Veronica persisted.

Robin didn't want to say Jonathan hadn't seemed all that interested to start with, so instead, she pasted a weak smile on her face and nodded, "I'll take care of it, Veronica."

The rest of the day passed happily. All the girls were being especially nice to Robin, and some of the boys even came over to look at her pin. Jonathan didn't look, but he did hold up *The Westing Game* from his seat across the room and made an okay sign.

At lunchtime all the AKGs sat together at a table, basking in their newfound celebrity. They pretended not to notice the whispers and stares that came their way.

"So what's new?" Lisa asked casually, taking a bite of her pasta salad. Her mother, who was a caterer, packed leftover pasta salad for Lisa almost every day. Robin didn't see how she could look another noodle in the face.

"We are." Kim giggled. "I can't tell you how many girls asked if we're taking new members."

"I told you there's no rush." Veronica's gaze swept the lunchroom. "We haven't left out anybody important."

Jessica cleared her throat. "There's a girl in my room who's nice."

"Who's that?" Lisa wanted to know.

"Sharon Anderson." Jessica craned her neck

so she could see over the heads of the milling students. "She's over there, with the short brown hair." Jessica pointed to a table several rows away, where a girl wearing glasses was reading a book while she ate her lunch.

Veronica glanced at Sharon, then turned back to the AKGs. "We can wait on her."

Candy looked in Sharon's direction and nodded vigorously. "You're right, Veronica."

"And let's not take any members unless all of us agree," Kim said.

"Good idea." Veronica nodded approvingly. "It's got to be unanimous."

"What does *unanimous* mean?" Candy asked, putting another cookie into her mouth.

"It means all of us agree." A frown was forming on Veronica's face. "Do you have to eat all those cookies, Candy?"

"Cookie Candy," Natalie giggled.

Candy stopped midchew. "Why shouldn't I?"

Veronica looked her over critically. "You've put on a few pounds. We don't want your weight to be awesome, you know."

All the girls laughed at this except Candy. She shoved the rest of her cookie into her brown lunch sack.

"I'm just telling you this for your own good," Veronica continued. "Every time you feel like eating something, think of Gretchen Hubbard."

Robin's eyes wandered over to where Gretchen was eating alone at a corner table. As if she felt her stare, Gretchen looked up at Robin. Then she put her head down and continued eating.

Gretchen stayed at the edge of Robin's mind all afternoon and it somehow seemed natural when Gretchen spoke to her as they were getting ready to go home that afternoon. The room had just about cleared out, with only a few kids left milling around. "Could I see your AKG pin?" she asked shyly.

Robin was both surprised and embarrassed. "Uh, sure," she said, fumbling as she unpinned it. Silently, she handed it over to Gretchen.

Gretchen handled it carefully, as though it were one of the crown jewels. Finally she gave it back. "Nice."

Veronica came up to them. "I designed it myself," she said.

Both girls looked up with a start at the sound of Veronica's voice. "What are you doing back here?" Robin asked stupidly.

"I was looking for you." Then she turned to Gretchen. "So you like the pin."

Gretchen looked like a trapped animal. "Yes."

"You know, Gretchen," Veronica said thoughtfully, "there may be a way for you to get into the AKGs."

"What?" Robin questioned, startled.

Veronica silenced her with a glance. "Of course, you'd have to prove that you were worthy."

"What would I have to do?" Gretchen asked eagerly.

"I'm not sure yet," Veronica said. "I'll get back to you on it." Then she nodded at Robin. "Let's go."

They left Gretchen standing there, her mouth hanging open. "What in the world were you talking about?" Robin demanded the second they got out of earshot.

Veronica's eyes crinkled with laughter. "I don't know, but wouldn't it be funny if we could get Gretchen to think she had a chance to get into the club?"

Robin wanted to yell, "No, it wouldn't," but she knew her protest could be the very thing to set Veronica in motion. Instead, she just shrugged and said, "I guess." And then she immediately changed the subject.

Robin was sure that Veronica had forgotten about Gretchen when she didn't mention her for the next couple of days. But then, while they were in the locker room dressing for gym, Veronica motioned the AKGs together and whispered, "Watch this."

She strolled over to Gretchen, who was zipping up her gym shorts with some difficulty. "Gretchen," she said, loud enough for her friends to hear, "I've been thinking about what we talked about the other day."

"You mean, joining the club?"

Veronica nodded. "Of course, you'd have to prove to us that you were sincere."

"How?" Gretchen asked excitedly. She looked like an overgrown puppy with a chance for a home.

Robin wanted to turn away, but she couldn't. She was only vaguely aware of her fingernails digging into her hands.

Veronica looked almost imperceptibly at her friends and then whispered to Gretchen, who first shook her head, then nodded.

Coach Brown blew his whistle, hustling the girls outside for a game of medicine ball. Without the other AKGs seeing her, Robin desperately wanted to say something to Gretchen. She furtively moved toward Gretchen, but before she could get close enough to whisper, the Coach touched her on the shoulder. "No dawdling, Miller!" he boomed and pushed her through the door.

Robin spent an excruciating twenty-five minutes. To the unknowing eye, it would seem that she was playing medicine ball, but really she was just waiting. She felt the same as she would have before a test, or in the dentist's office. Just waiting. Every once in a while Robin looked over at Gretchen, who refused to meet her eyes. Then, when the class was almost over and the girls were sprawled out on the grass, listening to Coach's announcements, Gretchen raised her hand.

Coach Brown peered at her over his glasses. "Yes?"

Gretchen stood up. "Coach, uh, I want to show the class my tumbling act."

"Your tumbling act?" he repeated.

Robin closed her eyes.

"Yes, I've been practicing."

The coach was nonplussed, but he glanced at his watch. "We have a minute or two before we're dismissed. Go ahead."

Gretchen moved slowly to the front of the class. She stood there for a moment, looking heavier and more awkward than ever. Then she got down on her hands and knees and did a somersault. As she lopsidedly rolled over, her fat thighs quivered like melting Jell-O. The edge of her underpants, caught in the elastic of her shorts, winked out at the class.

Veronica had been whispering to some of the girls, who snickered and passed on the joke to whoever was sitting next to them. By the time Gretchen righted herself and tried a cartwheel—her thick legs never even left the ground—a couple of the kids were stuffing their hands in their mouths to hold in the laughter, while others didn't even try to hide their hilarity.

Coach Brown didn't know exactly what was going on, but he knew enough to be angry. "That's enough, Gretchen. I don't know why . . ." The bell clanged noisily and everyone got up and ran indoors, laughing and screaming.

Robin knew she should be mad at Veronica, but her fury was directed at Gretchen, who was walking toward the locker room, her head down.

"How could you do that?" she yelled at Gretchen. A few of the other stragglers turned and then looked away.

Gretchen looked at her with tired eyes. "Veronica said she'd let me into the club."

"She won't. Don't you know that?"

Gretchen was gazing over her shoulder and Robin whirled around. There stood Veronica, observing the whole scene. "Can I be an AKG now?" Gretchen asked simply.

Veronica joined them, her voice dripping with fake sincerity. "I don't think so, Gretchen."

"But why not? You said . . ."

"Yes," Veronica interrupted, "but when I

saw you up there, I realized I couldn't let you in."

"Why?" Gretchen asked, confused.

Veronica stood right in front of her and emphasized each word. "Because . . . you're . . . gross."

All the color drained from Gretchen's face. She stood there stupidly for a minute, and then pushed past them into the locker room.

Now Robin turned angrily toward Veronica, who was looking after Gretchen with an amused grin on her face. "Veronica, that was a horrible thing to do."

Instead of responding directly, Veronica just reached out and ruffled Robin's hair. "Come on, Curly. Wasn't it funny? Gretchen trying to do a cartwheel?"

"Why? Why did you have to do it?" Robin insisted.

Veronica shrugged. "I did it because she's fat Gretchen Hubbard." And with that Veronica started toward the locker room. Then she turned back to Robin, who was as still as a stone. "Better hurry, Robin. Mrs. Volini hates it when we're late from gym."

Robin stood alone for a few seconds. Then she took a deep breath and followed Veronica into the locker room.

C H A P T E R
SIX

"I couldn't believe it," Lisa said, daintily putting a potato chip into her mouth. "How could she be so dumb?"

"Too bad no one had a camera." Kim grinned.

Robin sank uncomfortably into the plush velvet chair in Veronica's living room. The AKGs were supposed to be having a club meeting, but so far all they had talked about was the way Gretchen had made a fool of herself that afternoon. After gym, Gretchen had told Mrs. Volini she wasn't feeling well and had gone to the nurse's office, not to be seen for the rest of the afternoon. Robin didn't blame her. She would have feigned illness, even death, to get out of that room full of staring faces.

"No one's going to mess with the AKGs now," Kim continued with satisfaction.

"Not that they would have anyway," Natalie put in.

Jessica took a small sip of her cola and then said in her quiet way, "It wasn't a very nice thing to do."

Veronica turned to her pleasantly. "What did you say, Jessica?"

Now Jessica's voice was barely audible. "It was kind of mean. Wasn't it?"

"Well, I thought it was funny," Candy said importantly, putting down the brownie she was about to bite into. "She looked like . . . a dancing hippopotamus."

Lisa put her hand over her mouth to keep from spitting out her drink. Then, choking back her laughter, she said, "Oh wow, like those hippos wearing tutus in . . . what was that movie?"

"*Fantasia*," Natalie supplied through giggles.

"Gretchen couldn't be one of them . . . they were graceful," Lisa corrected to screams.

"See, Jessica, it was funny," Veronica said, her tone even. And Jessica nodded.

"Wouldn't you like to see Gretchen in a leotard?" Candy continued, trying to top her hippopotamus analogy. She wasn't used to people laughing at her jokes.

Veronica broke up at the thought and then added, "I'd even like to see you in a leotard, Candy."

Candy flushed, but continued smiling while the others, including Robin, roared.

That set them off. They started trying to outdo each other with word pictures—Gretchen in a bikini, or swinging from a trapeze while the people below cowered in fear that she'd fall on them.

At first Robin didn't feel very good about laughing, but the girls were being so silly— and funny—she couldn't help herself. Besides, she figured, if Gretchen was dumb enough to get up and do a somersault in front of the gym class, maybe she deserved what she got.

By the time Robin arrived home, she had decided to forget about Gretchen Hubbard. She took the image of Gretchen standing miserably outside the locker room and filed it away with other unpleasant memories, not to be thought of again.

"How was school today, honey?" her mother asked as she browned some onions for her spaghetti sauce.

"Fine," Robin answered automatically.

"Anything special happen?"

Robin shook her head. "Not a thing." Robin observed her mother for a second, her loose dress not entirely concealing her well-padded body. She knew her mother had been chunky when she was a girl. Had anybody ever made fun of her?

Robin went to her room and started her homework. When Mrs. Miller called her to the telephone, she had the sinking feeling that Gretchen was on the phone, waiting to yell at her. That was silly, she knew, but her heart was beating rapidly as she picked up the receiver in the living room.

Relief, which flooded over her when she heard Jonathan's voice, was immediately followed by a different emotion—nervous anticipation. "What's up, Jon?" she inquired, doing her best to sound nonchalant.

"I finished the book," he said.

"Oh good. I'm almost finished, too."

"We should get together and talk about it," Jonathan suggested.

Get together? Robin's mind raced. They could probably do all that was necessary over the phone, but she wasn't about to point that out. Clearing her throat, she said, "Sure. When do you want to do it?"

"How about tonight? Will you be done reading?"

Robin considered. "If I get on it right now, I can probably finish before supper."

"All right," Jonathan said agreeably. "Do it and I'll come over tonight. If that's okay," he added politely.

"It's okay." It's more than okay, she thought, but to Jonathan she said only, "Why don't you come around seven-thirty?"

Robin flew into the kitchen and told her mother Jonathan would be coming over later. She tried to act calm but Mrs. Miller had an amused smile on her face when she gave her permission. "This is just for homework, right?"

"Yes, it is," Robin said with dignity as she turned toward her bedroom. She hated it when her mother thought her activities were "cute."

Mrs. Miller must have gotten the message. When she told her husband at dinner about Jonathan's visit, she acted as if it was the most normal thing in the world and mildly asked Robin if she would like to use the sun porch so they could have some privacy. Robin cautiously said yes. She glanced sideways at her father to see if he was going to make a joke, but he was too busy wolfing down his spaghetti.

Robin stayed in her school clothes, but she did attempt to do something with her hair. As usual, it was a battle between her and her curls and the curls won. She stared broodingly into the mirror and wondered if she was always going to look like Little Orphan Annie.

Rummaging around in her sweater drawer, Robin found the lipstick that she hid there for special occasions. It was called Pink Blush and it was so pale it could hardly be seen—except by her mother. No matter how lightly she outlined her lips, Mrs. Miller invariably squinted at her and said, "Robin, are you wearing lipstick?" "Lipstick" was said in the same tone of voice her mother might have mentioned bat's blood. Of course, there were occasions when Robin scooted by her mom unseen. Before she could decide if tonight might be one of those nights, the doorbell rang and Robin shoved the lipstick back into her sweater drawer. She hoped to whisk Jonathan onto the sun porch so he wouldn't have to talk to her parents. But by the time she got to the living room, Jonathan was there, his hands shoved in his pockets, saying hello to Mr. Miller. "How're your folks?" her father was asking.

"Hi, Jon," Robin said, quickly entering the room. "Dad, we've got to get started."

"Fine, don't let me stop you," Mr. Miller replied, looking only the tiniest bit hurt.

Robin motioned Jonathan onto the sun

porch. She promptly shut the door behind her, but there was a knock, and her mother opened it immediately. Good thing I didn't wear the lipstick, Robin thought to herself.

"Can I get you kids something?" Mrs. Miller was asking in her friendly way. "There's cookies. Or pie left from dessert."

Robin rolled her eyes, but Jonathan seemed interested in the offer. "I'd like some cookies."

"Good." Mrs. Miller smiled. She left, leaving the door wide open.

"So, did you finish?" Jonathan asked, settling himself in on the couch and throwing *The Westing Game* down next to him.

"Yep." Robin hoped Jonathan had liked the book. She thought it was great. She knew she should have the courage of her convictions and come right out and say that, but she decided to hear his opinion first.

"Boy," Jonathan began, "I couldn't believe how many twists and turns this thing had. I couldn't put it down. You sure picked a good one," he added admiringly. Robin breathed a sigh of relief.

By the time Mrs. Miller returned with milk and cookies, Robin and Jonathan were heavily engaged in a discussion about the merits of *The Westing Game*. Jonathan remembered to say thank you, and after her mother left, Robin got up and closed the door.

They spent about half an hour figuring out what they were going to say in class. When they were finished, Robin waited anxiously to see if Jonathan would get up to leave. Instead, he asked if he could have some more milk.

"Sure," Robin said, relieved that he wasn't going quite yet. When she returned, she noticed Jonathan looking around the sun porch.

"You sure have a lot of books," he commented. "All these, and the ones in the living room."

"Yes," Robin said carefully. Jonathan was such a sports nut, she wondered if he thought people with all these books were weird. But Jonathan merely said, "When do you have time to read them all?"

Robin settled back into her mother's armchair. "They're mostly my parents' and they read all the time."

"That's nice." Jonathan sounded a little wistful. "My dad doesn't read at all. He says, 'Why waste time reading when you could be doing something?'"

Robin didn't know what to say to that. Reading was such an important thing in her house, so paramount to her parents, she couldn't imagine Jonathan's father scoffing at it. She wished Jonathan would change the subject, and he did.

"So," he said, drumming his fingers against

the arm of the sofa, "I suppose this Halloween party is a costume thing."

Robin nodded. "I haven't decided what I'm going to be yet."

"How's it going to work? Are the girls going to invite the boys?"

Robin knew this was the moment she should try to put in a plug for Veronica. "Uh-huh. You know," she stumbled, "there's someone who'd like to ask you."

Jonathan studied the bookcases. "Yeah?"

Robin chose her next words carefully. "Yes, but, well, I think she wants to be sure you'd go with her before she says anything."

Jonathan's eyes were still averted, his voice low. "I'd go with you, Robin."

"What?" Robin said, shocked.

Now Jonathan repeated his acceptance a little more strongly, looking right at her. "I said I'd go with you."

Robin just stared at Jonathan, aghast. He thought she'd been talking about herself! How could she embarrass him—both of them—by saying she meant Veronica? Frantically, she tried to think of the right thing to say, while Jonathan sat there, waiting.

"Uh . . . that would be great, Jonathan," she finally squeaked.

Jonathan gave her a full-fledged smile. "I'd like it, too, Robin." Then he glanced at his watch and said, "Well, I should be going. I biked over here and it's getting dark."

Robin walked him to the door and said goodnight in a daze. As she walked past the living room to her bedroom, her mother called, "Did Jonathan leave, Robin?"

"Yes. He's gone." And I'm dead, she thought as she shut her door. She flopped on her bed and stared up at the ceiling, trying to figure out where things had gone wrong. There seemed little she could have done to save the situation.

Robin knew that she should get right up and call Veronica, but she stayed bound to her bed as if held there by chains. There was no way Veronica was going to understand that this had all been a horrible misunderstanding. No— tomorrow she would throw herself on Jonathan's mercy, tell him the whole story and explain that Veronica wanted to be his date for the party.

Robin grabbed her Angora cat and held it close. After all, Robin thought, any boy would want to be Veronica's date. Yet a small voice was whispering in her ear, "It's you he wants to go with. He likes *you*." Robin fell asleep, still hearing the words.

C H A P T E R
SEVEN

The next morning Robin crawled out of bed, feeling tired and cranky. She had fallen asleep with her clothes on, but had a dim recollection of her mother helping her undress while she stood there and yawned. Once in her pajamas, she went back to dreams punctuated by angry faces, although whose she could not quite remember.

As Robin brushed her teeth and splashed water on her face, the fog in her head began lifting. Then last night's events came rushing back and Robin sat shakily on the edge of the tub. No wonder I had those nightmares, Robin thought to herself. She debated which would be worse, her dreams or today's confrontations.

Candy was not in her usual seat on the bus this morning and Robin sat alone at the window, barely aware of the hubbub around her. She kept trying to work up some enthusiasm for her idea of last night—tell Jonathan the truth and give him the good news about Veronica—but none came. Robin was glad no one was paying any attention to her as she blinked back a tear.

As Robin clattered off the bus, the first thing she saw was Veronica and Jonathan talking in the schoolyard. He's telling her about the party, she thought wildly and stood stock-still.

"Hey, move it," a boy behind her yelled, and other kids started pushing past her.

Slowly, she began making her way toward Veronica and Jonathan. As she walked, she couldn't help noticing how nice they looked together, both tall, with almost the same color hair. Veronica didn't seem to have the butterflies Robin usually felt when she was talking to Jonathan. She was smiling confidently, gesturing with her hand. That's a good sign anyway, Robin thought. Veronica wouldn't be smiling if she knew Jonathan had asked Robin to the party.

"Hi, Robin," Jonathan greeted her first.

Veronica turned and made a face at Robin that clearly said, "Get lost," but Jonathan was already asking, "Did I leave my copy of the book at your house?"

"Gee, I didn't notice," Robin murmured with a sideways glance at Veronica, who was all attention.

"Maybe it fell behind the couch," Jonathan suggested. "Check for me, will you?"

Robin nodded, but avoided his eyes.

When it didn't appear that Robin was going to say anything else, Jonathan moved uncomfortably away, barely acknowledging Veronica's " 'Bye, Jon."

The second Jonathan was out of earshot, Veronica asked, "Why didn't you tell me Jonathan was coming to your house? What happened?"

Suddenly, Robin's plan to talk to Jon first didn't seem feasible. Now that Veronica knew about his visit, she'd be like a dog with a bone. I might as well tell her, Robin thought to herself. But, looking into Veronica's expectant face, she didn't know where to begin.

"What's wrong?" Veronica asked, a puzzled look on her face. "You look weird."

"I . . . I don't feel well," Robin replied.

"Do you want me to go with you to the nurse?"

"No, I'm just going to class," Robin replied and hurried away before Veronica could question her further. The classroom was empty, and Robin slid into her seat and put her head down on the desk. Maybe everyone will leave me alone, she thought. Maybe Mrs. Volini will tell me I have to go home. Forever.

An insistent voice whispered in her ear, "Robin, did you talk to Jonathan about the party?"

Robin nodded, her head still in her arms.

Veronica shook her. "Well, what did he say?"

Robin half sat up and said, "It was nothing much. I'll tell you at recess."

Veronica frowned. "All right. If you're really not feeling well, I guess I can wait."

The room was beginning to fill and Veronica took her seat, still staring at Robin curiously. Robin made herself sit up straight. She had bought a little time. Maybe she *should* try and get to Jonathan. Surely, if she fixed things, Veronica couldn't be too mad.

But as the morning wore on, through math and social studies, rebellious thoughts began forming in Robin's mind. Why couldn't she be the one to go with Jonathan if she wanted? Why did everything have to be Veronica's way? She was being disloyal, Robin knew, but she couldn't remember wanting anything as much as going to that party with Jon.

A crack of thunder and a burst of rain splattering against the windows brought Robin to attention. Rain! That meant no recess, so she had another reprieve. Yet Robin found time dragging.

Finally the sixth grade lined up for lunch and Robin hadn't even crossed the threshold into the cafeteria when she felt a hand on her shoulder. "Why didn't you wait for me?" Veronica hissed.

Robin shuddered as she backed into the narrow corridor that led to the storage room. "I don't know."

"What's with you, Robin? I started talking to Jonathan this morning because you've been moving so slow. I was asking him about our math homework, but if I'd known you saw him last night, I could have worked the party into the conversation."

Robin decided to just get it over with. "Veronica," she began hesitantly, "things didn't quite go the way I expected."

"What do you mean?"

"Well, I brought up the party," Robin continued, her words moving quickly now, "and I said someone wanted to ask him, and he thought I meant me. Before I knew what was happening, he said he'd be glad to take me."

"You're kidding?" Veronica looked at her with unbelieving eyes.

"I swear, I'm not even sure how it happened," she finished limply.

For once Veronica was speechless. They just stared at each other for a few seconds, then Veronica found her voice. "You're just going to have to tell him you can't go."

"I know."

"I can't believe you even let it get this far," Veronica said viciously.

Robin didn't say a word. She just nodded.

"There he is." Veronica pointed toward the line, where Jonathan stood by himself, waiting to get a tray. "Just go over there and tell him it was all a mistake."

Robin turned like an automaton and moved toward Jonathan, who smiled when he saw her coming. "Hey, Robin, what's up?"

Robin meant to start in on her explanation, but she heard herself saying, "Not much."

They just stood together for a few seconds until Jonathan finally asked, "Do you want a tray?"

"No." He was so sweet, with his hair falling onto his forehead. She couldn't tell him. She didn't even want to. Robin gave him a sickly smile and went back to Veronica.

"Well?" she asked impatiently.

Robin felt as if someone else was speaking. "I didn't do it."

"Why not?" Veronica's eyes narrowed.

"Veronica, I think he wants to go with me," Robin began nervously. "Really, I know he does, so why don't we just leave things the way they are and . . ."

Veronica looked ready to explode. "But Jonathan's going to be my date. He's the only boy I want to go with."

"I should have told you," Robin said desperately, "but I like him, too."

"When did you decide that?" Veronica's voice was so shrill that several students turned and looked at them.

"I've liked him for a while."

"I don't believe you. You just decided that when he asked you to the party." She paused. "Or did *you* ask him?"

"No," Robin answered, confused. "Honest . . ."

"*Honest?* What a joke."

"It wasn't the way you think," Robin tried to explain.

"I thought you were my friend."

"I'm your best friend." Now Robin's own anger was rising.

"You deserve a best friend like Gretchen Hubbard."

"Leave Gretchen out of it."

Veronica cut her off. "You took an oath to be

loyal to your club sisters. Either you go back to Jonathan right now or you won't have to worry about him being your date. You'll be out of the club!"

Robin felt as if she were outside her body, watching two furious girls facing each other. Suddenly, she wasn't mad anymore, or scared. It was as though she had been turned to ice.

"Well," Veronica was insisting, "which is it?"

She fumbled with her AKG pin, then shoved it into Veronica's hand. "You can't boss me around." Robin was amazed her voice sounded so cool. "I couldn't care less what you want me to do." She left Veronica with her mouth open and walked out of the cafeteria. It was totally against school rules to leave the cafeteria without a pass, but Robin didn't care. She had just broken the biggest rule of all by talking back to Veronica. Nothing the principal could do to her would be worse than Veronica's revenge.

CHAPTER
EIGHT

Robin felt as though a door had slammed shut in her face. She was never sure how Veronica had accomplished it so quickly, but by the time school was over, all of the AKGs were passing her silently, their expressions hard.

At first she hadn't been too upset, calming herself with the thought that she and Veronica would make up and the whole thing would blow over. But three, then four days passed, and Robin became uncertain. After that the laughing started.

It began in the schoolyard. Robin had been walking by the AKGs, who were huddled together in a group, when a shriek of laughter rang out. Turning slightly, she saw Kim whisper something to Veronica, who smirked at

Robin and nodded.

From then on, anytime Robin walked by two or more of the AKGs, the laughing and giggling started. She tried to avoid the girls, but since most of them were in her class, that was almost impossible. If she read aloud, she could hear the soft titters behind her. When she got up to sharpen a pencil, the snickers began again.

The word was out to the rest of the sixth grade girls, too. With an opening in the AKGs, they didn't want to incur Veronica's wrath—or blow their chances by talking to Robin.

So Robin went to school alone and came home alone. At recess she would stand and watch the fifth grade kickball game as if it was the most interesting thing in the world. During lunchtime she sat as far away from the AKGs as possible, and tried to avoid looking at them. Every once in a while, though, she did look and they seemed to be having a wonderful time. Robin hated waking up in the morning, knowing it was going to start all over again.

One morning Mrs. Volini announced the names of the partners that would be giving their book talks the next day. Robin's heart sank when she heard her name and Jonathan's called. She knew it was inevitable, but the last thing she wanted to do was stand up in front of the class.

Jonathan had been as friendly as ever, but soccer practice had started after school and he was busy with the team. Besides, it appeared to Robin that things were different with the boys. They never seemed aware of who was in and who was out with the girls. Or if they knew, they didn't care. The girls might be living in another country, or in outer space, for all the attention they paid.

So Robin wasn't really surprised when, after checking on her readiness for the talk, Jonathan asked, "Are we still going to the Halloween party?"

His tone was tentative. Perhaps the news that she was a pariah *had* filtered down to the boys. Robin rubbed her finger on the dirty lunch table where she'd been sitting alone. "I guess not."

"What happened?"

She sighed. "It's a long story. I had a fight with Veronica."

"Oh" was all Jonathan said. "I'm sorry," he added quietly.

"We'll probably make up soon," Robin replied without much conviction. "But I don't think it'll be before the party."

Jonathan shook his head. "You girls are always fighting about something."

"I guess we are."

Robin was so nervous the next day that her stomach hurt. She was terrified that somehow the AKGs would disrupt their report, and she almost warned Jonathan, except she couldn't find the words. Staring hard at the back wall, Robin gave the title of their book and waited for the giggles to start. But maybe in deference to Jonathan, the girls let the whole thing go by without any whispers or laughs. Finally, it was over and shaking with relief, Robin went back to her desk. A note was sitting on top of it, which she slowly unfolded. "Her hair is red, she's as flat as a bed, Robin is going to wish she was dead."

Tears started to form in Robin's eyes, but with a strength she didn't know she possessed, she refused to let them fall. She was beginning to wish she was dead already.

When she dragged home that afternoon, her mother was sitting at the dining room table, waiting, with her favorite chipped china teapot and two cups.

Why couldn't she be a latchkey child who came home to an empty house instead of having a mother who worked weekends and nights? Robin thought.

"Robin, come sit and have a cup of tea with

me," Mrs. Miller said, motioning to an empty chair.

"Mom, I don't even like tea."

"Indulge your mother," Mrs. Miller said with a tired smile.

Robin slid unwillingly into the chair. Her mother could make her sit, and even drink tea, but she couldn't make her talk.

"How about a nice piece of bread pudding?" Mrs. Miller asked as she poured the tea. "I just made some, fresh."

"No thanks."

"Robin," her mother began again, taking a deep breath, "we have to talk."

Robin put two lumps of sugar into her tea. "What about?" she asked, unwilling to make this easy for either of them.

"You've been moping around here for at least two weeks. Veronica has disappeared and no one else calls either. When I ask you what the problem is, you say, 'Nothing.' "

"What are you, the police?"

"Don't use that tone with me," her mother said angrily. Then she forced a note of calmness into her voice. "I want to help."

"Nothing's wrong," Robin insisted.

"Then, where's Veronica?"

"I thought you didn't like Veronica," Robin countered.

"You know I always believed Veronica exercised undue influence over you," Mrs. Miller said slowly. "But I don't dislike her personally."

The tears that Robin had stopped earlier in the day began to well up once more, and this time they began to spill over. "Well, you won't have to worry about her influencing me any more because we aren't speaking." She wiped away her tears with the back of her hand, furious that she had revealed so much.

"I thought it was something like that." Mrs. Miller rubbed the rim of her cup with her thumb. "I know you don't want to talk about it, honey, but it might make you feel better if you did."

If her mother had been insistent, or prying, Robin might have regathered her resolve, but something in her soft tone made the hardness inside Robin crack. The whole sorry story spilled out, mixed with Robin's tears.

"Oh, Robin, I'm so sorry," Mrs. Miller said, stroking Robin's head, which was buried in her hands. "It was wrong of Veronica not to understand."

Robin didn't bother answering that. What did it matter if Veronica was wrong? She could do anything she wanted.

"I just can't believe all the girls would follow

her like sheep," Mrs. Miller murmured as if to herself.

"Mom," Robin groaned, "you're the one who doesn't understand. Everybody does what Veronica wants."

Mrs. Miller shook her head. "Surely, not everyone."

Robin pushed herself away from the table and ran toward the safety of her room. She should have known her mother wouldn't have the faintest idea of how things worked.

Robin flung herself on her bed, wanting only to be left alone, but Mrs. Miller was right behind her. "Robin, do you want me to call Mrs. Volner? Or one of the other mothers . . . ?"

"No!" Robin screamed, lifting her head off the bed. "Don't you dare call anybody!"

Mrs. Miller put up her hands. "All right, all right, I was just trying to help."

"You can't help," Robin cried, burying her face in her pillow. "Just leave me alone."

Mrs. Miller stood silently in the darkened room for a few seconds and then softly closed the door behind her.

Strong sobs wracked Robin's body for a few minutes until slowly they faded away. Reaching into her jeans pocket for a crumpled tissue, she blew her nose and then lay quietly. How did she always manage to do the wrong thing, she wondered—first with Veronica, now with her mom. Mrs. Miller wasn't going to just forget about this, Robin was sure of that.

Going down to supper was almost as much an ordeal as giving her book talk. But when Robin, her eyes as red as her hair, finally came into the dining room, her parents tried to act as if nothing had happened. It was only at the end of a rather quiet meal that Mrs. Miller said, "Robin, Daddy and I know this is a bad time for you, but we'll give you some time to work it through without interfering."

"Maybe it'll all blow over, honey," Mr. Miller said optimistically, patting her hand.

Robin felt badly for her dad, who knew so little that he could still have hope. "Maybe," she said, trying to give him an encouraging smile.

Robin usually adored Saturdays, the one day when her mother allowed her to sleep late and then do whatever she wanted after she cleaned her room. But this Saturday stretched endlessly before her. She threw on jeans and a sweatshirt and wandered downstairs.

There was a note sitting on the kitchen table. "Robin," it read, "Mom's at work and I've gone to the hardware store. Maybe we can go to the museum when I get back."

Oh great, Robin thought as she threw some bread into the toaster, now her father was planning activities to keep her occupied. She gulped down her breakfast and scribbled a note for her father on the same sheet of paper. "Went for a bike ride."

The hot weather had finally broken and the first taste of autumn was in the air. Robin biked aimlessly for a while and then found herself heading toward Veronica's house as if she was on automatic pilot. But before she got too close, she squealed on her brakes and turned in the opposite direction. What would she do if she actually did see Veronica? She wasn't prepared to apologize and Veronica would want more than that anyway. She would want Robin to grovel.

Going nowhere in particular, Robin continued to ride, forcing her legs to push the pedals again and again. After about ten minutes, she noticed she was near the subdivision where Jessica lived and Robin resolutely decided to see if Jessica was home. Of all the AKGs, Jessica was the one who might be the least influenced by Veronica. For one thing, she wasn't in Mrs. Volini's room. For another, she was probably the nicest of the AKGs. Why, she had even come right out and said their treatment of Gretchen was mean, Robin remembered.

If Jessica hadn't been sitting on her front step, Robin might have lost her nerve, but there she was, playing checkers. To her surprise her opponent was Sharon Anderson. Bonnie, Jessica's beagle, was stretched out next to them.

Robin jumped off her bike and clutched the handlebars, willing Jessica to notice she was there. As if sensing her presence, Jessica glanced up. Then quickly she turned away, but Sharon nudged her and pointed to Robin. Robin just stood there, waiting, and finally Jessica whispered something to Sharon and walked over to Robin with Bonnie nipping at her heels.

"You shouldn't be here," Jessica said, nervously brushing her short hair.

"Jessica, I know Veronica is mad. . . ."

"She's *really* mad," Jessica said. "Anybody who talks to you is out of the AKGs." Furtively, she looked over her shoulder as if spies might be waiting to report her transgression.

"The whole thing's a mistake. I didn't mean for Jon to ask me to the party."

Jessica's eyes widened. "Jon asked *you*?"

The surprise on Jessica's face was mirrored in Robin's own. "Sure."

"Veronica said that you were acting like a . . . a go-between she called it. But instead of telling Jonathan good stuff about her, she says you were telling him all kinds of lies because you liked him yourself."

"That's not what happened," Robin exploded. "She's just mad because Jon likes me."

Jessica looked as though she didn't know what to believe. "Veronica told us you had broken the first rule of the AKGs: Be loyal to your club sisters."

"I know. She said that to me, too. But, Jessica, it wasn't like that."

"If you weren't loyal to Veronica, you wouldn't be loyal to us either," Jessica said, obviously repeating Veronica's words.

Robin felt utterly defeated. There didn't seem to be any way to make Jessica understand.

"Maybe," Jessica said, "maybe if you apologized to Veronica, she'd forgive you."

"Don't think I haven't thought about it," Robin answered, rubbing her thumb nervously against her bike handle. "But I'm not the one who's wrong. Veronica's always pulling this stuff. You saw what she did to Gretchen."

Jessica looked at her helplessly. "There's nothing we can do about that."

"If we all got together and talked to her . . ." Robin began hopefully.

"No way." Jessica shook her head. "No."

"You could bring it up with some of the other girls . . ."

"None of them would go for it. Not Lisa. Definitely not Candy. She already thinks she's Veronica's best friend. Besides," Jessica continued softly, "the girls think ragging you is fun."

"And what about you?" Robin said, looking at Jessica steadily. "Do you think it's fun?"

Jessica's face grew red. Before she could say anything, her mother appeared at the door. "Veronica's on the phone, Jess. Do you want to talk?"

"Yes." Without another word to Robin, she turned and hurried into the house. After a backward glance at Robin, Sharon went in, too.

Robin stood looking after her for a few seconds. Then she walked slowly on with her bicycle and once again began riding to nowhere in particular.

As the days passed, Robin was only conscious of how one faded into another. Get up, go to school, come home, do homework, go to sleep, get up . . . sometimes she felt invisible. An invisible person who went through the day without anyone except her parents really noticing her. Even the laughter had slowly stopped. It was as if she was so insignificant that she wasn't even worthy of their whispers.

Robin had hoped that Jessica would tell the others the truth, but apparently that hadn't happened. Or if Jessica had told, they didn't care. Lunchtimes were the worst, with everyone laughing and chattering away. Once Robin tried to join the table of sixth grade girls from Mr. Jacobs's room and, even though no one told her to get out, they hadn't exactly welcomed her either. Only the new girl, Sharon, smiled at her, but Robin couldn't think of anything to say to her, especially over the other girls' noisy talk. The smile cheered her a little, but the next day Robin went back to sitting by herself. Forcing herself on people who didn't want her just seemed like too much of an effort.

One morning at recess, Robin was so desperate, she actually went up to Gretchen, who was standing alone, watching the boys practice soccer. "Hi, Gretchen," she murmured. The words felt uncomfortable in her mouth.

"What is it, Robin?" Gretchen said warily.

"How are you doing?" Robin asked, for lack of anything else to say.

Not meeting Robin's eyes, Gretchen said only, "Okay."

"I was wondering, Gretchen. Maybe you'd like to come over this afternoon. We could listen to some records, or do our homework . . ." Robin's voice trailed away when she saw Gretchen shaking her head.

"I don't want to."

"You don't?" Robin repeated, her voice filled with surprise. It was hard enough to ask Gretchen over. She certainly didn't expect to be turned down.

"No." Gretchen still pretended to be watching the soccer game. "You never asked me over when you were friends with Veronica."

Robin knew that she probably had that coming, but Gretchen's words tied her heart in a knot anyway. "I just thought that since we both had some free time . . ." she started to explain.

Gretchen's laugh was bitter, so unlike the sweet laugh Robin remembered. "You'd spend it with a dork," Gretchen finished for her.

"It's not like that," Robin protested.

"You mean you wouldn't come back if Veronica snapped her fingers?" Gretchen finally turned her gaze to Robin.

In her heart Robin knew the answer to Gretchen's question. Gretchen must have known it, too. "I like being by myself," she said. "I'm used to it now." Standing up a little straighter,

Gretchen turned and headed back into the school building.

Robin slumped against a nearby tree and then slid to the ground. She had to hand it to Gretchen. Robin was sure that she'd fall over herself to be friends, but Gretchen didn't need her. Somehow she had learned to be by herself, to even like it. Robin wondered how long it took to learn that lesson. She pulled a clump of grass from the ground and flung away the blades one by one. It looked as though she was going to find out.

NINE

Mrs. Miller watched warily as Robin hung her jacket in the hall closet.

"Mom, I'm not some bug under a microscope. What do you think you're going to see if you keep staring at me like that?" Robin asked crossly.

Shaking her head, Mrs. Miller sat down on the living room couch. She motioned Robin to come sit next to her, but Robin flung herself into the recliner chair, pushing out the footstool with a hard upward kick.

"Robin, I think the time has come to do something about this situation of yours."

"Like what, Mom? Take out an ad in the Forest Glen *News* and see if we can hire me a friend?"

Mrs. Miller's expression was somewhere between exasperation and desperation. "I'm tired of your sarcasm and I'm tired of you moping around the house," she said wearily.

Don't you think I'm tired of it, too? Robin asked silently.

"I'm going to insist you take a class after school, Robin. Art, drama—I don't care what it is. I've gotten folders on them all." She reached over and rummaged around in her tote bag, took out several brochures and handed them to Robin.

"I'll take a look," Robin said without much enthusiasm. She was about to drop them on the end table when her mother broke in, her voice firm.

"Robin, this isn't negotiable and this isn't something you can put off. By the time you go to bed, I want a decision. Then tomorrow I'll sign you up."

"Oh, Mom," Robin said automatically, but secretly she was relieved that her mother had taken charge. She could pretend indifference, even dislike for Mrs. Miller's plan, but she had to admit going somewhere—anywhere—after school was appealing.

As soon as her mother went into the kitchen, Robin began looking at the brochures. The one from the Forest Glen park district consisted of several mimeographed sheets stapled together. It described all kinds of different activities: ceramics, weaving and painting among them. Robin carefully read the description of the painting class. It sounded nice enough and she loved drawing, but art was something Robin preferred to do alone, without anyone looking over her shoulder.

Putting the park district flier behind the others, she glanced at the next brochure. Artistic lettering proclaimed *Miss Juliet's School of Ballet*. A grainy black-and-white photograph featured several girls dressed in tutus, their toes pointed, arms gracefully arched over their heads. Robin didn't have to think twice about ballet school. Just looking at the picture made her toes ache. She flung the brochure away and watched the dancers waft to the floor.

Robin rifled through the rest of the folders. A photography class offered at a local studio didn't have much appeal, and if Mrs. Miller thought Robin had the least interest in learning to cook, she was sadly mistaken. But a glossy folder with red-and-white lettering on the cover, proclaiming *Beech Street Theater*, did catch her eye. Inside were listed creative dramatic classes for different age groups and levels of experience. Beech Street—Robin thought the name sounded familiar. Then she remembered that Bobby Glickman, the boy in her class who did commercials, took classes at Beech Street.

Robin leaned back in the comfortable chair. She had never thought of herself as an actress, although she had taken the lead of *Frosty, the Snowman* in the third grade holiday pageant. If she did say so herself, she'd been an excellent Frosty. She hadn't forgotten one line. The memory of the applause that greeted her curtain call made Robin smile. Maybe going to a dramatics class wouldn't be so bad.

Still, she didn't want to appear too anxious. Robin waited until her mother came home from work that evening to inform her of her decision.

"That's wonderful," Mrs. Miller enthused as she sat heavily on Robin's desk chair and examined the Beech Street Theater brochure. "The beginners' group meets Wednesday afternoons, so you've only missed one."

"Mom," Robin cautioned from her bed, "I don't want you to get your hopes up about this. I mean, don't expect me to find a bunch of new friends."

"There're going to be kids from all over Forest Glen, and from other suburbs, too," Mrs. Miller said in her practical way. "How do you know you won't find some people you like?"

Robin sighed. "Beech Street is just something to do. Can't we let it be that?"

"It can be anything you want, Robin. Just try to have fun with it, okay?"

By Wednesday, Robin was already regretting her decision. She was sure she'd get up onstage and make a fool of herself. Great, she thought. New people to start laughing at me.

Nevertheless, she dressed carefully in her best oversize sweatshirt, the one decorated with ribbons, and the jeans she had been saving for parties. She figured there was no point in saving them anymore. Before school started, she found Bobby Glickman and told him she was going to be taking a class at Beech Street. "What's it like?" she asked shyly.

"It's neat!" Bobby exclaimed. A short wiry boy with cropped black hair, Bobby always had a grin on his face. Being in television commercials had done a lot for his popularity, but success hadn't gone to Bobby's head. He was friendly, always laughing and joking, much to Mrs. Volini's displeasure. He never talked about being on TV unless someone else brought it up first.

"I'm in the beginners' class," Robin told him.

"I was in that last year. A guy named Gregory teaches it. You do improvisations, and read scenes from plays. You'll like it."

"I will?" Robin asked doubtfully.

Bobby gave her a funny look. "If you didn't think so, why did you sign up?"

"It's kind of hard to explain, Bobby."

Robin went to her seat and took out her math homework. She glanced over at Jonathan, who smiled and waved. Jon was just as nice as ever, but he hadn't made any special effort to hang out with her since their study date. Robin had had a fantasy that Jonathan would beg to be her boyfriend—a real boyfriend who took her to the movies and out for pizza—but he hadn't even called. Robin had heard her father talk about a run of bad luck. Now she knew what that meant.

After so many endless days, it felt funny to have one pass quickly. Especially a day she didn't particularly want to end. When the bell rang at a quarter to three, Robin dawdled a little, clearing off her desk. Even though she knew her mother was waiting for her in the car, she decided to stop at the bathroom. Casually swinging open the door, Robin was horrified to see Veronica standing alone, combing her long dark hair.

Robin's immediate impulse was to run, but Veronica had already spotted her in the mirror A wave of homesickness swept over Robin. She didn't want to be heading off to the Beech Street Theater. She wanted to be somewhere with Veronica, laughing at nothing special, basking in the warmth of their friendship.

At this moment, alone with Veronica, Robin realized she would do anything to end their awful fight. Maybe if she said she was sorry, said it nicely and quickly, they could go back to the way things used to be.

But before Robin could open her mouth, Veronica turned toward her, a smug look on her face. "Well, well, if it isn't Curly. Getting ready for your acting debut?"

"How did you know?" Robin asked, dumbfounded.

"Candy asked Bobby what you two were talking about this morning, so he told her. And she told me."

"Yeah, what if I am going to Beech Street?" Robin asked in what she hoped was a careless tone.

Veronica smiled with fake sympathy. "Poor Robin. You don't think that's going to work, do you?"

"I don't know what you mean," Robin replied stiffly.

Veronica put her comb back in her purse and snapped it efficiently shut. "Get involved in some silly drama stuff so you can forget that you don't have any friends."

"That's not why I'm doing it."

"Oh, you're an actress all of a sudden." Veronica hooted.

Now Robin was starting to get mad. "What's with you, Veronica? Why do you have to be such a creep?"

"Me? You started this whole thing, Robin."

"And you lied to the other AKGs. I never told Jon bad things about you."

Veronica's eyes were bright. If Robin didn't know better, she might have thought that Veronica was going to cry. "You think you can have everything, Robin, but you can't."

The words swam around Robin's head. She didn't know what Veronica was talking about. But before she could ask, Veronica continued, her voice shaky, "I was supposed to be your best friend. You even vowed to be loyal to me. And then you go after Jon, just because you knew I liked him."

"I've told you a million times that it wasn't like that," Robin insisted, but Veronica just ignored her protests.

"Well, I hope you have fun at your stupid drama class, or whatever it is. Because otherwise you're not going to have any fun until high school."

At that moment Robin hated Veronica. "You really think you run things, don't you?"

"Yes, I do." She pushed past Robin, and hurried out into the hall.

Robin moved unsteadily to the sink and turned on the faucet. She splashed some cool water on her face, and then stared into the mirror. After that horrible exchange, she half-expected to look different somehow. But except for two bright pink spots on her cheeks, her reflection was the same.

She knew her mother must be waiting impatiently for her, so Robin quickly finished up in the bathroom and rushed to the parking lot. Mrs. Miller was standing outside the car, scanning the schoolyard. When she saw Robin, her irritation was mixed with relief. "Where were you? I thought I missed you."

"In the girls' room."

"Are you all right?" Mrs. Miller asked, concerned. She looked Robin over carefully. "You're flushed."

"I'm okay," Robin reassured her, but she wished she could tell her mother to just drive home. What was the point of joining Beech Street? Veronica was right—it was a diversion that would have no bearing on her real life. But explaining that to her mother would be harder than going along with the plan. As Mrs.

Miller rattled on about how much fun she was going to have, Robin looked out the window and kept her mouth closed.

Classes for Beech Street Theater were held in an unused school building that also housed the community theater group. Knowing she was late, Robin rushed inside and followed the signs to the auditorium, where the beginners' acting class was already sitting in a circle on the stage.

A tall skinny man with hair long enough to be pulled back in a pony tail was talking to eight or nine kids who all seemed interested in whatever he was saying. Robin moved quietly down the aisle until the teacher noticed her and motioned her up on the stage. Self-consciously, Robin climbed the steps, at the same time looking to see if she knew anyone. But before she could separate the faces in the crowd, the man said, "You must be Robin. I'm Gregory."

"Sorry I'm late," she murmured.

"No problem. I was just telling the kids about improvisations."

Robin moved to an open space on the floor and sat down quietly. She directed most of her attention to Gregory, but she also examined the kids more closely. Sharon Anderson, that friend of Jessica's, was there and so was a girl

Robin thought she recognized as Lisa's cousin.

"Improvisation is one of the greatest feelings in the world, when it's going right," Gregory was saying. "I give you a situation, and you act it out. Just make it up and see where it takes you."

Robin felt herself growing warm. Just make it up? How do you do that? She glanced around the circle, but none of the other kids seemed particularly upset by the prospect. One or two even looked as if they might spring up and start improvising any minute.

"For instance," Gregory continued, "let's say you're astronauts who just landed on the moon. What do you do? What do you say? Put your imaginations to work!"

Robin was doubtful. She didn't think she had all that much imagination. Certainly not enough to let it run wild, as Gregory so enthusiastically put it.

"But before we start doing improvs, let's do a few mind-stretching exercises. I'd like everyone to close their eyes."

Robin obediently shut her eyes, then opened them into a squint. She wanted to make sure everyone was following instructions.

"Now, each of you pretend you're a cat. Just pretend it in your mind. You're moving, eating, but whatever actions you're visualizing, try to put yourself in the cat's place. Feel what it's like to be that animal."

This is silly, Robin thought. Besides, she was allergic to cats. Her nose was itching just thinking about having fur all over her. But trying to get into the spirit of things, she pretended she was a sleek Siamese cat, first stretching, then walking over to a goldfish bowl and hungrily watching the gleaming fish swimming in circles. By the time Gregory had them open their eyes, she was feeling very catlike indeed.

"Fine," Gregory said approvingly. "Now, why don't we all stand up?" There was a shuffle of feet as everyone rose. "Let's pretend we're trees."

The group looked at each other blankly. What did trees do? Most of the kids just stood around awkwardly, though a few stuck their arms over their heads, simulating branches.

Gregory roamed around the stage. "Well, you don't look very much like trees."

Robin agreed. What they looked like was a bunch of kids with their arms above their heads.

"Close your eyes," Gregory commanded. "First, decide what kind of tree you'll be. An apple tree weighed down with fruit? A Christmas tree with presents under it? Take as much space as you need."

Feeling like a fool, Robin decided to be the maple tree in her backyard. It was autumn and she was losing her leaves. She shook her arms a little as the wind caused the leaves to fall, one by one. Then a funny thing happened. Robin started to think about how the tree must feel as its gloriously colored leaves began to drift away. It was very sad knowing that it would soon be naked, with snow covering its branches and trunk. Robin the Maple Tree tried to stand a little straighter, brave in the knowledge of what she would face as the temperatures plummeted. A voice whispered in her ear. "You make a very majestic tree, Robin," Gregory said.

Being praised for her treelike behavior was probably the dopiest thing that had ever happened to Robin, but she smiled nevertheless.

The rest of the class time was spent in more active pursuits, with the kids pretending they were cars and planes and boats. When someone disdainfully said, "This is the kind of stuff we did in kindergarten," Gregory laughed. "You're right, you know. The whole thing about acting is to get back to that time when you were absolutely free to act just like you felt. That's what little children do. The best actresses and actors hold on to that quality, so they can let the characters they're playing come out."

"But when are we going to do some real acting?" one of the boys wanted to know.

"Soon. These are just warmup exercises that we do before we even get to the improvs. But believe me, if you can pretend you're a tree, that's step one."

As Robin walked toward the door, she was surprised and pleased when Sharon came up to her and said, "So how did you like it?"

"It was interesting," Robin replied. "Actually, it was fun."

"I know," Sharon agreed. "I thought it was crazy at first, but it's kind of neat to make things up."

"I wonder what we'll be next week? Mountains, maybe."

"Probably just hills." The girls exchanged grins. "Well, I've got to catch my bus," Sharon said, suddenly looking shy. "See you."

" 'Bye." Robin looked at Sharon's receding figure thoughtfully. She seemed nice. And the class had been good, too. For almost an hour, Robin had been so busy pretending she was something else that she hadn't had a smidgen of time to think about her problems. Next time the girls hassled her, maybe she should start buzzing around the room like an airplane. A giggle escaped at the thought.

Bobby Glickman was coming out of his class. "What's so funny?" he asked her quizzically.

Robin sobered up immediately. "Nothing."

But when Mr. Miller, who was reading in the car, asked Robin how things went, she smiled broadly. "I was the best tree in the class."

CHAPTER
TEN

Life wasn't perfect, but to Robin's great relief it was getting better.

One big difference was Sharon. The day after they spoke at Beech Street, Sharon had caught Robin's eye in the lunchroom as Robin was making her solitary way to a table.

Sharon made a slight motion with her head, indicating an empty seat, and after a few seconds' hesitation, Robin had joined her and a couple of the girls from Mr. Jacobs's room. Like the last time she sat at that table, Robin got a couple of strange looks, but no one actually shooed her away. After a few uncomfortable seconds, the table regulars turned back to their own conversation.

"What exactly did you do?" Sharon asked in

u whisper, so the others couldn't hear. "To make them freeze you like that, I mean."

"I got on the wrong side of Veronica Volner."

"Yeah, Jessica told me a little about it, but then she clammed up. Something about not telling club secrets."

Robin opened her container of milk. "Are you a good friend of Jessica's?"

"She lives around the corner from me and sometimes we do our homework together." Sharon's eyes were cool and clear behind her glasses. "But mostly she's busy with the AKGs."

After that Robin ate lunch with Sharon. They weren't friends, not exactly, but just knowing she would see Sharon at lunch made things easier for Robin.

The AKGs still ignored her, except for one horrible moment when Mrs. Volini stepped out of the classroom. Amanda Baxter was the room monitor, and despite her feeble attempts at keeping order, the sixth grade was up for grabs.

Robin watched warily as Lisa sauntered over to her. Making sure the other AKGs were watching, she asked, "Robin, what kind of a tree are you anyway? One with Dutch Elm disease?"

Robin sat still, shocked, wondering how Lisa could have known about the exercise at Beech Street. Then she remembered the girl in the class who she had thought was Lisa's cousin. The AKGs must have asked her to spy for them! Mrs. Volini returned before Robin could say anything to Lisa—not that anything had come immediately to mind.

But by the next session of drama class Robin had thought of plenty. She had marched right over to Lisa's cousin and informed her that if she ever—ever—told Lisa anything that went on at Beech Street, she would go right to Gregory, tell him the whole story and get her kicked out of class. Robin wasn't sure Gregory would go along with her, but apparently the girl believed her. After that she had studiously ignored Robin—and Robin was pleased she'd stuck up for herself.

Another very good thing that happened was a date with Jonathan. He had biked over to her house one Saturday and they had ridden downtown, stopping for hot chocolate at The Hut. Even though it hadn't happened a second time, Robin savored the memory.

But it was Beech Street, the promised reward for everything else she had to put up with, that highlighted Robin's week. Robin didn't kid herself. When it came to improvs or pantomimes, she knew her acting was stiff and inhibited. Once Gregory asked her to play a dog walker trying to deal with a group of unruly dogs, and when she was done, he informed her she looked more like a boxer trying to fight off several opponents. But he said it with such a friendly smile that it didn't really matter.

She was much better when he gave them actual lines to read. The beginners didn't attempt whole plays. Gregory just gave them scenes to practice. Robin had the most fun playing Scrooge in *A Christmas Carol*. Sharon had come up afterward and said, "You were so mean, I wanted to hit you."

A dog walker or Scrooge, it really didn't matter to Robin as long as for an hour a week she didn't have to be herself.

But Robin was brought back to reality whenever her path crossed Veronica's. After the initial shock of their meeting in the bathroom wore off, Robin thought long and hard about what Veronica had said that day. Despite all the mean comments, what stuck in Robin's mind was Veronica saying "you think you can have everything." What did she have that Veronica didn't? She would have loved to ask, but Veronica was more distant than ever. She looked through Robin as though she were a ghost.

When Robin's mother asked her one rainy afternoon if she was going to dress up for Halloween, she had shrugged. Halloween meant just one thing to her: the party the AKGs were having. Even though no one was speaking to her, she couldn't help but hear about it. Waiting in line, or in the locker room, the AKGs talked loudly about who was invited and what they were wearing.

Robin was dying to know if Jonathan was going. Sharon had heard from Jessica that Veronica had given up on the idea of individual dates. Instead, it was going to be the AKGs, two or three prospective members and a group of the most popular boys. Robin was sure Jonathan had gotten an invitation. Finally, she just gathered up her courage and asked him if he was going.

Jonathan shook his head. "We have to go to Ohio and visit my grandmother. She fell and broke her arm. It's going to be a really nothing Halloween."

Would he have gone otherwise? Robin wondered. But she couldn't make herself ask anything more. It was enough that fate and his grandmother's arm were making him leave town for the weekend.

Halloween was on a Saturday. It dawned bright and crisp, just the weather she had always wished for when she was a little kid and rarely got. Usually it was freezing and there was nothing worse than getting all dressed up as a fairy princess and then ruining the whole effect with a heavy jacket.

Robin was sitting up in bed, rubbing her eyes, when her mother knocked softly to announce her presence. "Robin, Mrs. Remington just called. She wants to know if you'll take Remy and Dennis trick-or-treating tonight."

Robin swung her feet off her bed. She sometimes baby-sat for the Remington kids and they were no picnic. Rambunctious boys of four and six, they caused Robin enough trouble when they were supposedly asleep. She certainly didn't want to drag them around the neighborhood when they were dressed up, hyped up and full of sugar.

But a plan was forming in Robin's mind. "She'll pay me, right?"

Mrs. Miller shrugged. "I suppose. I don't think she expects you to do it just for the love of Remy and Dennis."

Robin returned her mother's understanding smile. "Maybe, if Sharon will come with me, I'll do it."

"Give her a call," Mrs. Miller said heartily. "It could be fun."

Her mother was so transparent, Robin thought as she threw on her robe. Anything to get her out of the house with some company her own age.

Robin was nervous as she looked up Sharon's number in the Forest Glen phone book. This would be the first time they had seen each other outside of school or Beech Street. But Sharon readily agreed to take on the Remington boys and split the money. Robin didn't tell Sharon the rest of her plan, for fear she might change her mind.

Promptly at seven o'clock, Sharon showed up, wearing her regular clothes and a rubber gorilla mask. "Trick or treat," she mumbled through the slit of a mouth.

"Sharon, I'd know you anywhere," Robin said dryly. She opened the door wide. "Come in."

Sharon pulled the mask off her face, leaving her brown hair sticking up in spikes. "Where are they?" she said, looking around the living room.

"They'll be here soon enough," Robin said. "Want a Snickers bar?" She motioned to the basket of candy on a table at the side of the door.

"No." Sharon shook her head. "Are you going to bring a bag for trick-or-treating?"

Robin shrugged. "Why not? If we're making the effort to go, we might as well reap some of the rewards." There was a momentary silence as Robin realized that Sharon was the first girl who had visited her house in a long time. It felt funny. Her mother, who Robin was sure would have broken the ice with some warm greetings and cookies, had gone to an early movie with Mr. Miller, leaving Robin to play hostess alone. Finally she said, "Why don't we sit down?"

But before Sharon could go into the living room, the doorbell rang again. This time Robin let in a harried Mrs. Remington and two tiny hobos.

Robin quickly made the introductions all around. When Sharon told the boys how cute they looked, Remy replied, "I hate you," then Dennis promptly broke into tears.

"Oh dear," Mrs. Remington said, more frazzled than ever. "Maybe this wasn't such a good idea after all, but I promised Remy months ago he could go trick-or-treating at night and my husband and I just have to go to my sister's Halloween party."

"What are you going as?" Robin inquired politely.

"Princess Di."

Sharon and Robin exchanged glances. Mrs. Remington was short, wide and had black frizzy hair.

"I've got a crown and scepter," she explained while trying to comfort Dennis, who was now clinging to her leg.

"That should help," Robin agreed.

"Well, I'll just let you get going," Mrs. Remington said, disengaging herself from Dennis. "Bring them home around eight. Their grandmother will be there then." With that, she escaped, bringing new howls from Dennis.

"Now, no more crying," Robin said sternly. "Just let me get my mask and we'll go." She picked up her old plastic Cinderella mask from the hall table.

"You have cracks in your face," Dennis screeched after she put it on.

"What?"

Sharon started laughing. "That plastic's so old, it's cracked."

Robin glanced in the hall mirror and through the tiny eye holes she could see what Sharon meant. She hadn't looked at it very closely when she brought it up from the basement. "Those are just wrinkles," Robin informed Dennis. "Cinderella needs a face-lift."

"Oh," Dennis said, subdued. "Grandma had one of those."

Sharon put on her own mask, which impressed the boys mightily.

"So, here we go," Robin said as she led

them outside. "A gorilla, Cinderella and two hobos."

"We're street people," Remy informed her with dignity.

Robin had a feeling this was going to be a very long night.

For almost an hour, Sharon and Robin had led the boys up and down sidewalks, ringing doorbells, filling their candy bags and stopping for compliments, when Robin casually said, "I have an idea."

"What's that?" Sharon asked, pulling off her mask.

"Veronica's house isn't far from here. Why don't we go over and see what the AKG party is like?"

"Why would we want to do that?"

Robin squirmed. She didn't think she was going to have to draw a picture for Sharon. "You know, just to see," she finished lamely.

"If it's not too far, I guess it would be okay." Sharon's voice was colored with indifference. "But I think our street people are getting tired."

"No, we're not!" Remy bellowed.

"Well, it's good that you're not," Robin said, patting him on his porkpie hat. "Because now we're going to a house where there's a party. We can't go in, but we can watch through the windows."

"Like spying, right?" Dennis said, skipping along.

"Uh, not exactly," Robin said uncomfortably.

"No?" Sharon muttered, but followed anyway.

As Robin expected, the party was being held in the rec room. The music was playing loudly, so loudly that little Dennis began dancing around as soon as he heard it, coming up the walk. Robin whisked the boys off behind the bushes, where they could see but not be seen.

"Let's ring the doorbell," Remy was saying, pulling at Robin's arm.

"No, we can't do that." Robin shook her head.

"Do they have candy in there?" Dennis's lower lip trembled.

"They have Candy Dahl," Sharon murmured.

The boys were making such a fuss, Robin knew that they'd better not stay long or they might bring the whole party outside. All she needed was for Veronica to see her and Sharon with their dates—two boys under seven.

"All right, we'll go in a minute," Robin promised, but instead, she moved closer to the rec room window, kneeling down so she could peer in. The AKGs and several of the hopefuls danced with boys dressed as pirates and rock stars.

Kim and Natalie were dressed in matching silk pajamas, the brightly colored kind that were sold in Chinatown; and they both looked adorable. Jessica was dressed as Peter Pan, Lisa was a hippie and Candy was made up as a rather plump cat—or some kind of animal.

Veronica was a queen. Her long dark hair flowed down her back and she wore a sparkling crown. Were they diamonds? Robin wondered. Most likely, they were rhinestones, but they still looked real. A long velvet dress added to the elegant illusion. Robin was willing to bet that Veronica looked a lot more like royalty than Mrs. Remington did.

Robin watched as Veronica went up to one of the boys dressed as a pirate and asked him to dance. She snuggled next to him and Robin was only glad it wasn't Jonathan's shoulder she was leaning against.

"Just how long are we going to stay here?" Sharon asked impatiently.

Robin tore her eyes away from the dirty basement window. "I guess we can go."

"Yeah, let's go," Dennis agreed. He hitched his pants uncomfortably. "I have to make . . ."

That was enough to get Robin moving. They hustled the boys home and then walked back to Robin's house. Sharon was quiet the whole way.

"I should call my mother," Sharon said, stuffing her gorilla mask in her pocket.

Robin pointed her toward the kitchen phone and then flopped down on the living room couch, her mind still on the party. It looked like fun, but Robin felt surprisingly good about not being there. Even though she'd never been to a party with boys, she could imagine what was going on. There'd be all kinds of whispering and gossip. The girls would meet in twos and threes in the bathroom to talk about who liked who and what was being said. Robin didn't miss that part of it.

"My mom will be here in a few minutes," Sharon said, sitting carefully in Mr. Miller's well-used recliner chair.

"Do you want something to eat? My mom bakes a lot. There's sure to be something around."

Sharon motioned to her bag of candy. "I've been eating too much of this stuff already. It's making me kind of sick."

Robin knew Sharon was unhappy about stopping at Veronica's, but she hoped they wouldn't have to talk about it. Before she could lead the conversation in another direction, however, Sharon brought it up.

"I have to tell you, Robin, I think snooping around Veronica's was tacky."

There wasn't much Robin could say to that.

She was probably right. But because Robin liked Sharon, she tried to explain. "I just wanted to see what the party was like. And I wanted to see how it felt not to be there."

"So how did you feel?"

"I thought I'd get really jealous, because I was missing something." Robin gave a small shrug. "But I didn't feel much of anything."

"Well, that's good, I guess," Sharon said, running her hand along the edge of her trick-or-treat bag.

"It's hard, Sharon," Robin said honestly. "Veronica was my best friend for so long that sometimes I really miss her . . . even though I know she's not a very nice person." Robin's voice was so low that Sharon could barely hear her.

"Why is she like that? I haven't been here that long, but some of the things I've seen her do . . ." Sharon rolled her eyes.

"I've been trying to figure that out. It's weird, but Veronica's kind of like a roller coaster. The dangerous stuff is what makes her fun."

"If you say so," Sharon conceded. "But if you ask me, Veronica Volner is trouble, pure and simple."

Trouble? Sharon didn't know the half of it.

CHAPTER
ELEVEN

The drama class was acting out a scene from *Peter Pan* when Robin noticed a fashionably dressed woman walk into the room. Their class had never had a visitor before, and Robin was distracted as the woman slipped into a seat in the front row of the auditorium.

But, after glancing into the darkened theater once or twice, Robin went back to her script.

When the class was drawing to a close, Gregory clapped his hands and asked the kids to sit down. Obediently, they formed their usual circle around him and listened expectantly.

"You may have been wondering who our visitor is." He motioned the woman up from the audience. "This is Ms. Morrison and she's from an advertising agency in Chicago. She'll tell you why she's here."

"Hello, everyone," Ms. Morrison said, coming into the middle of the circle. "I'm here today because our advertising agency is going to be doing a public service announcement. Does anyone know what that is?"

Sharon raised her hand. "They're like commercials, but instead they say things like 'Don't drink and drive' or 'Only you can prevent forest fires.' "

Ms. Morrison smiled warmly at Sharon. "Exactly right. They are television messages that we hope will give viewers important information. Our agency is going to produce one about how bad drugs are for kids. I'm sure you've all heard that." When everyone nodded, Ms. Morrison added, "Naturally, we're gong to need some children to appear in this PSA, which is a shortened name for public service announcement."

The class started buzzing and Ms. Morrison motioned with her hands to quiet them down. "I can't say which of you—if any—will be chosen, but I'll be in touch. Anyway, it was fun to watch you. Even if we can't use some of you for the PSA, I hope we'll meet again."

After Ms. Morrison left the auditorium, Gregory tried to get everyone's attention. The kids were so busy whispering to each other that it was a little difficult. "Hey," he said, raising his own voice. "Can I have some quiet, please?" Reluctantly, the class turned toward him. "I know this is exciting news, but remember, Ms. Morrison is looking at other drama classes, too, and she only needs one or two kids. All right?"

"I still think she'll pick one of us," Robin insisted to Sharon as they waited in front of the building for Mrs. Miller to come get them after class. Sharon was going to have dinner at her house.

"Why?" Sharon rubbed her hands up and down her arms to ward off the brisk breeze.

"She didn't have to tell us what she was here for, did she?"

"No," Sharon admitted.

"And she could have sneaked out as quietly as she came in."

"So?"

"So, why would she waste time explaining PSAs if she didn't have someone in mind?" Robin folded her arms, proud of her powers of deduction.

"I don't know. But why pick one of the beginners when she could have someone like Bobby?" Sharon said practically. "He's the professional actor."

Robin couldn't argue much with that. Ms.

Morrison probably did want Bobby. But that night, lying in her bed, she thought about how neat it would be if Ms. Morrison wanted her.

For the next few days, Robin picked up the phone on the first ring. When she came home from school, she asked right away if she had gotten any calls. But as time passed and nothing happened, Robin figured that Sharon was right. Besides, there was something happening at school that was attracting her attention. The AKGs weren't getting along.

At first Robin thought it was her imagination. Was that really a dirty look Lisa shot at Candy as they waited in line to go to the library? Her suspicions were aroused again as she observed a flurry of notes passed between Kim, Natalie and Veronica. None of them looked happy.

Soon the other girls in Mrs. Volini's class were talking about it, too, and they were talking about it to Robin. It had happened slowly, but Robin wasn't quite the outcast she once was. As near as Robin could figure, as the girls got less excited about the AKGs, they forgot about ignoring her. The AKGs still avoided Robin, but it was no longer unusual for the other girls to check about a homework assignment or ask her to be on their relay team during gym. So when Amanda Baxter leaned across the aisle and whispered something, it was no big deal. But what she said was a surprise. "I saw Kim and Veronica fighting in the library."

Robin couldn't help but be interested. "What about?"

"I didn't hear everything, but Kim was telling Veronica just because she was president, she couldn't decide everything. If the AKGs break up, I might still start a club. What do you think?"

"Don't ask me. I don't have a very good track record with clubs." Robin turned back to her work.

Robin, her mind still on the AKGs, dawdled on the way home from the bus stop. She was surprised when she saw her mother standing in the doorway, waving to her. "Robin, where have you been?" Mrs. Miller was dressed in her good suit.

Robin stared at her mother. "I told you I was taking the second bus so I could go to the library."

"Well, you'd better hurry up and change. Your Ms. Morrison called."

"What?"

"You heard me," she answered briskly, hustling Robin into the house and to her room. "The people from the advertising agency want to see you over at Beech Street at four-fifteen."

"It's a quarter to four now!" Robin wailed.

"I know." Mrs. Miller was practically undressing her as if she was a baby.

"Do they want me?" Robin asked, her voice muffled in the sweater that was being pulled over her head.

"I don't know. They just said to have you there." Even the normally calm Mrs. Miller was flustered. She threw a capful of shampoo into the tub she was drawing instead of bath foam, but made Robin get in anyway. "Bubbles are bubbles," she insisted, but Robin thought taking a bath in shampoo was the height of ick. If she hadn't been in such a hurry, she never would have done it.

"What am I going to wear?" Robin called to her mother, who was rifling through her closet with a furious intensity.

"A dress. They said to wear a dress."

A dress? Robin couldn't remember if she had any dresses.

Her mother appeared in the doorway and Robin slunk modestly down under the bubbles. "There's this."

"Oh, Mom," Robin groaned. It was the dress Nonnie had brought back from England —dark green corduroy with a dainty floral pattern and a white lace collar. It was pretty enough in an old-fashioned way, but Robin had felt like a dope on the two occasions she had been forced to wear it. "It's too sweet," she protested.

Mrs. Miller shook her head, loosening a few strands from her French roll. "You look adorable in it. Really, Robin. I know it's not your favorite, but Ms. Morrison said a dress and . . ."

"All right." Robin scowled. "Throw me a towel."

Robin had never gotten dressed so quickly: first underwear, then the dress, and finally green knee socks and some patent-leather party shoes that were a little too tight. She was done, except for her hair.

"Comb it in the car, Robin," her mother said, grabbing their coats.

"I can't even make it look decent in front of a mirror. How can I fix it in the car?"

"Do the best you can."

Robin combed all the way to Beech Street, but her curls bounced around as much as ever. If I lose this part because of my stupid hair, Robin vowed, I'm shaving myself bald.

Robin rushed into the auditorium just five minutes late. She was motioned up on the stage by Gregory, who was standing with Ms. Morrison and two other men Robin had never seen before. Her mother hovered in the background until Gregory asked her to come up on the stage, too. He shook her hand and introduced them all around. Robin shyly said hello to the men, one of whom worked at the ad agency. The other was from the drug prevention group that was sponsoring the public service announcement.

"Robin, how nice you look," Ms. Morrison said, taking her in with a practiced eye.

"Thank you," she replied quietly.

"Would you mind doing a reading for us?"

Gregory put a *Peter Pan* script in her hand and pointed out one of Wendy's speeches. "Try that one."

Robin was relieved to see it was a part of the play she was familiar with. Though her voice was shaking a little when she began, by the time she finished, she thought it had gone all right.

Ms. Morrison was nodding at the two men when Robin looked up. "I think we have some good news for you, Robin. We'd like you to be in our spot. If that's all right with your parents, of course."

"It sounds like a wonderful opportunity." Mrs. Miller smiled at Robin, who was too stunned to say anything.

"And I have another surprise," Ms. Morrison continued. "Tony Moroni is going to be in it, too."

"Tony Moroni, the rock star?" Robin breathed.

"Yes. We weren't sure we could get him, but he's confirmed for tomorrow." Ms. Morrison turned to her mother. "I'm sorry for the short notice, but it's the only day we could get Tony. Will Robin be able to miss school?"

"I guess it will be all right for one day. I'm sure I couldn't live with Robin if I said no," Mrs. Miller added dryly.

"You won't have much to say. Maybe just a line or two. I'll give them to you tomorrow."

"I had no idea Robin was so talented." Mrs. Miller looked at Robin with respect.

"Well, part of it was how well Robin read," Ms. Morrison said slowly, "but the hair helped."

"My hair?" Absently, Robin patted her curls.

"Yes. I'm sure you know, Robin, Tony Moroni has curly red hair, too, so we thought it would be fun if all the kids in the PSA—there are two more of you—had red hair, too."

Robin couldn't believe it. Her hair had gotten her the part. As Nonnie always said, "Go figure."

Ms. Morrison gave her mother directions to

the studio where the PSA was being shot and then added a wonderful bit of news. "We're not doing dress-up clothes, after all, Robin. Just wear jeans and a white shirt and we'll have a sweatshirt there for you with 'No Drugs!' printed on the front."

Robin went home in a daze. Her mother chattered eagerly about tomorrow's shoot, but all Robin could do was nod. As soon as they walked into the house, Robin took the phone into the hall closet and called Sharon, who squealed with delight.

Then she called Bobby. Although Bobby was glad for her, it was not just his congratulations she wanted. Robin knew Bobby was likely to tell most of the kids in their class the reason she wasn't in school. Calling Bobby was a little sneaky, but all Robin could feel was satisfaction when she hung up the phone.

"Where's my movie star?" Mr. Miller was pounding on the door of the closet.

"Daddy!" She tumbled out into his arms. "I'm not a movie star."

"Soon to be," he assured her, giving her a big hug. They walked into the kitchen, Mr. Miller's arm around Robin's shoulders. "What are you doing, Lois?" he asked Mrs. Miller, who was staring blankly into the open refrigerator.

"Trying to figure out what to make for dinner. Stars still have to eat."

"And so do their parents," Mr. Miller agreed expansively. "But we have reason here to celebrate. Let's eat out."

"What a good idea." Relieved, Mrs. Miller shut the refrigerator door. "Robin, you should pick."

"Pizza Village," Robin said promptly.

Mr. and Mrs. Miller exchanged looks. Pizza Village was not their favorite place.

"You said I could pick," Robin reminded them.

Mr. Miller laughed and tousled her hair. "So we did. Who cares about a little indigestion when we're so proud of you. Besides, someday I expect you to buy us steaks."

Dinner was fun. Robin was so keyed up that by the time she crawled into bed, she doubted she'd ever fall asleep. But as soon as her now-lucky red curls were down on her pillow, Robin was off, dreaming about singing in a rock band with Tony Moroni.

Whenever Robin thought back on her day at the television studio, it was almost like remembering a dream. Her mother had brought her there promptly at nine o'clock and Ms. Morrison had introduced her to the other kids in the PSA—a boy about ten with copper colored hair, and another boy who was slightly younger, a real carrot top. Ms. Morrison was showing them their places on the set when Tony Moroni blew in, dressed in jeans and a satin jacket, followed by several people who he introduced as his *entourage*. Robin made a note to look that word up when she got home.

Tony was everything Robin hoped he'd be. "Star" was written all over him, but he was nice, too. He said hi to the three of them in a friendly, natural way and then laughingly added, "They should call us the Red Menace." He turned to Ms. Morrison and added, "Great name for a rock group."

The actual shooting of the spot flew by. The director seated them on the carpeted boxes and then they practiced a couple of times with Tony talking about how the worst thing you could do was muck up your body with drugs. Robin and the two boys didn't have much to do except nod and say at the end, "No drugs," but then Ms. Morrison came over with a suggestion. "Robin, when Tony says, 'You know what I mean,' I want you to look right at him and answer, 'We sure do, Tony.' Got that?"

She had a line! When they ran through it again, Robin looked into Tony's beautiful eyes and said it perfectly. She did it again, once the cameras were actually running. After the director said, "It's a wrap," over the intercom from his booth into the studio, Tony chucked her under the chin and said, "Good work, darlin'." Robin thought she might faint.

Then there was just time for autographs and Polaroid photographs taken with them all together before Tony left, waving. Ms. Morrison smiled after him and said, "He sure is something, isn't he?" Robin couldn't argue with that.

The next morning Robin debated whether she should put on her "No Drugs!" sweatshirt, which Ms. Morrison had let her keep. She decided it would be too obvious, but she slid the photograph carefully in an envelope and put it in her backpack.

Mr. Miller had insisted on driving her to school, saying she deserved the star treatment, and her mother laughingly agreed. When she stepped out of the car, the AKGs were clustered in a tight-lipped group, not speaking but watching her carefully. Veronica, in particular, had a sour look on her face. That didn't stop a number of the other girls, and boys, too, from coming up to her and asking what Tony Moroni was really like.

Robin basked in the attention. Sharon had already told a lot of the kids that Robin had a picture of herself taken with Tony and they were clamoring to have a look. Like her dad, Jonathan kidded her about being a movie star, but he carefully showed the photograph around while Robin recounted her experience at the studio. All that day there was a steady stream of visitors to her desk, and surrounding her in the schoolyard and the cafeteria.

To her surprise, one of her lunchtime visitors was Jessica.

"Hi, Robin," she said quietly, but she kept her eyes on Sharon.

Robin didn't feel especially friendly. "Hi."

"Some of the kids said you have a picture of Tony."

Robin looked at Sharon, who shrugged. Robin took the envelope off her tray and silently handed it to Jessica.

Jessica studied it. "I heard he called you darling."

"Yes."

"It must have been neat," Jessica said, handing it back.

"It was a rare moment," Robin agreed. "Kind of like this one."

Robin and Sharon had a long talk about the day's events while they were doing their homework together at Robin's house.

"And Lisa came over when we were leaving

the building," Robin recounted. "Just like nothing had ever happened. I couldn't believe it. Of course, she waited until the other AKGs were gone."

Sharon munched a chocolate chip cookie. "What about Candy? Did she say anything on the bus?"

"Not a word. She walked right past me like always." Robin rubbed at the pink-and-white checks on the wall.

"That figures," Sharon said, stretching herself into a more comfortable position on the floor. "She's Veronica's slave. But they can't hold out forever," she added thoughtfully. "You're the star of the sixth grade."

"Not really," Robin said. "After all, there's Bobby."

"Who has Bobby Glickman ever costarred with but a box of cereal?"

Robin sat quietly for a minute, then decided she could be honest. "You know, Sharon, this is making me feel weirder than I thought it would. I mean, suddenly kids who didn't talk to me for weeks think I'm great. And the only reason I got picked was because of my hair color. If you'd been the redhead, it would have been you sitting next to Tony and I'd still be a geek."

Sharon seemed startled by this thought,

then she shrugged. "Hey, you got lucky. You might as well enjoy it."

Robin tried. When the PSA ran on television for the first time, Mrs. Volini asked her to get up and tell the whole class about the experience. This was something she might have dreamed about—the kids looking eagerly at her, asking her questions—but it all seemed kind of silly. Where had they been when she really needed their friendship? She felt happy only when Gretchen shyly told Robin she had looked good on television.

"Thanks, Gretchen." Swallowing deeply, Robin said, "I don't think you saw the picture of me with Tony. And the TV people gave me the sweatshirt I wore. Would you like to come over and see it sometime?"

Gretchen looked startled, then wary. "Maybe," she said, and hurried away. Robin could understand. She knew how it felt, not wanting to be hurt.

The last period of the day was library, a wonderful leg-stretching time when the students were allowed to roam pretty much at will while they picked out books. Robin was browsing through the mystery section when she noticed Lisa, Kim and Natalie in the corner, whispering and looking in her direction. She tried to ignore them, telling herself she must be used to their hushed conversations by now, but she couldn't deny the wormy feeling sliding through her stomach. Where was Veronica, she wondered, expecting her to join the group any second. But to her surprise, she spotted Veronica alone at a nearby table, engrossed in a book.

Robin turned resolutely to mystery hunting. Yet she knew Kim was behind her even before she felt the light tap on her shoulder.

"What?" she said, whirling around.

Kim's smile was nervous. "I didn't mean to scare you."

"You didn't," Robin said coldly. "What do you want?"

"I, well I mean, really we . . ." She nodded toward Lisa and Natalie who were still huddled in the corner. "We liked your speech, Robin."

This was not what she had expected to hear. "Thanks," she managed.

"And we've been thinking, the three of us, and Jessica, too, maybe we should start a new club."

"A new . . . but what happened to the AKGs?" Robin stammered.

"It was getting to be a drag," Kim informed her. "We're barely speaking to Veronica."

Robin's eyes darted in Veronica's direction.

For a second, their eyes locked, then Veronica turned back to her book. "You're not speaking to her . . . *either?*"

"I guess things did get a little out of hand with you," Kim acknowledged her point.

There was an embarrassed silence. Then Lisa and Natalie walked over to fill the void. Even though there were only three of them, Robin felt as if she was surrounded.

"I was just telling Robin our idea," Kim said, trying to sound bright.

Lisa was equally enthusiastic. "It could even be a Tony Moroni fan club."

"And that Sharon you've been hanging out with? She could join, too," Natalie added generously.

Robin couldn't believe it. Did these girls think they could just pick up where they left off, without even bothering to say they were sorry? But instead of demanding an apology, she tried to find out more about Veronica. "You don't want Veronica in this new club at all?"

"Hey, you of all people know how Veronica can be," Kim said, a little more confidently now.

"Really mean," Natalie offered.

"And s-o-o bossy." Lisa rolled her eyes. "And it was worse after she was AKG president. She was always telling us what to do."

I thought that's what you like about her, Robin said silently.

After another uncomfortable moment, Kim asked, "So how do you feel about a club?"

"I'll have to let you know." The trio seemed satisfied with that, and Robin excused herself to go to the bathroom. She was grateful to find the room empty, but Robin locked herself in a stall anyway. She knew she should have told them to forget their ridiculous club and leave her alone. But there had been so much fighting already. It was easier just to walk away.

To her own surprise, Robin kept quiet about the AKGs' offer. She didn't even tell Sharon, though she wasn't exactly sure why. She just wanted to think about it by herself.

She thought about it a lot. That was what she was doing Saturday, home alone, lying on her bed. Hearing the doorbell ring and thinking it might be Sharon, she flew to answer the door. There stood Veronica.

She marched into the living room, looking as confident as ever. Without any preamble she said, "I want our fight to be over, Robin."

This almost amused Robin. "Oh, do you?"

"It's gone on long enough," Veronica decreed.

Robin might have bought her sureness, but

she noticed the way Veronica rubbed her knuckle. She always did that when she was nervous. Knowing this wasn't as easy for Veronica as she pretended gave Robin confidence. "Because you say so?"

"Well, yes." Veronica looked surprised.

"I would have liked it to be over weeks ago, Veronica, but my opinion didn't count for much."

Veronica put on her familiar patronizing expression. "Come on, Curly, fights happen."

"Don't call me Curly. I hate it," Robin snapped.

"All right," Veronica recoiled. "But like I said, I think we should make up."

"Why should I? You know all the AKGs except Candy asked me if I wanted to start a new club."

She thought that surely Veronica knew about this defection. But from the way her superior smile crumbled, Robin realized Veronica had no idea things had gone this far.

"They did?" she whispered.

Robin nodded, savoring the moment.

"You're not going to do it, are you?"

"I haven't decided." Now it was her turn to act cool.

"Oh, don't, Robin. You could come back to the AKGs and everything would be okay again." There was a note of desperation in Veronica's voice.

"You think the others would stay in the AKGs?"

"If you stayed in, I bet they would. They really think you're a star or something," Veronica mumbled.

"The girls are really angry," Robin informed her. "I'm not even sure they'd be in a club with you."

Veronica didn't say anything, and Robin was afraid she had pushed her too far. Then Veronica murmured, "You could convince them."

"Well, maybe I could," Robin said cheerfully. "If that's what you're sure you want, for us to be club sisters."

"And friends." Veronica pushed the two words out.

Robin wasn't moved. Her mind raced as she tried to think of some way to keep her advantage. "It could happen. But you'd have to do something for me."

"What?" Veronica asked hopefully. "What do you want me to do?"

She needed an idea fast, but she didn't have one. Then, as she stood looking at Veronica, Robin realized she needn't give her an answer this minute. She could take all the time she wanted. Putting on the same bored smile that she was used to Veronica wearing, Robin told her the same thing she had told the AKGs: "I'll have to get back to you."

"But . . ."

She ushered Veronica to the door. "I've had lots of offers lately, Veronica. It's going to take time to sort them all out." She closed the door and gleefully said out loud, "And it's going to be fun."

C H A P T E R
TWELVE

After Veronica left, Robin went to her room and slammed the door. She hugged her Angora cat to her as she replayed the scene with Veronica over and over in her mind. Robin couldn't deny it; watching Veronica crawl was a heady feeling. And to think Veronica was willing to do even more to get back in her good graces! Robin leaned against her headboard, visions of all sorts of dire punishments dancing through her head.

She could make Veronica tell Luke the Puke Olson, the nerdiest kid in fifth grade, that she loved him. Or she could have her deliberately flunk a test. Veronica took a great deal of pride in her good grades, and so did Mrs. Volner. There were all sorts of possibilities—picking just one was going to be hard.

But first, Robin simply wanted to enjoy watching a nervous Veronica. It was strange being at school on Monday and seeing no one standing next to her but Candy. The other AKGs had formed their own knot, a friendly one though, and they all chorused hello as Robin walked by. Veronica just looked at her questioningly. Robin smiled, but didn't stop to talk to any of them. Instead, she went over to Jonathan, who was gathering his books, waiting for the first bell.

"Hi, Jon," she said cheerfully.

"You're in a good mood," Jonathan noticed.

"I've got a lot of things to be happy about," Robin agreed.

"For instance?" Jonathan was curious.

Robin strolled with him as they headed toward the school building. "Did you ever have a chance to get back at someone?"

"You mean, like revenge?"

"Revenge." Robin savored the word. "Yes, revenge."

"What's the deal?" Jonathan looked at her strangely. "You're not out to get somebody, are you?"

Robin didn't care for that look. Suddenly she didn't want to talk about this anymore. Fortunately, the second bell rang and Robin had to sprint to her seat before Mrs. Volini began taking roll.

As Mrs. Volini checked off names, Robin decided to forget about Jonathan and concentrate on her plan. When Mrs. Volini called out, "Hubbard," Robin turned her head in Gretchen's direction. As usual, Gretchen was sitting with her hands folded, her eyes looking straight ahead. Robin wasn't sure what punishment she was going to dream up for Veronica, but an apology to Gretchen was going to be in there somewhere.

After shoving her attendance book in the drawer, Mrs. Volini asked the class for their attention. "I have an announcement from the office. Tryouts for our annual holiday talent show will be held tomorrow afternoon in the auditorium. The sixth grade classes have been invited to watch so the participants can have an audience." Mrs. Volini looked up from her piece of paper. "I'm sure we have many talented people in our room. If you'd like to try out, let me know and I'll pass along your name and what you're planning to do to Mr. Jackson, the music teacher. He'll be doing the choosing."

Robin, who wasn't paying much attention, started when a note of folded paper appeared on her desk. Opening it tentatively, she saw it was from Kim. "Why don't you try out?" it said. "Maybe you could give a dramatic reading or something." It was signed *Kim* with a heart over the *i*.

Was Kim being sarcastic? But when Robin, her eyes narrowed, looked in Kim's direction, she was smiling and nodding.

Robin gave a small shrug and turned back to the front of the room. There was no way she was going to get up and audition for the talent show. She might audition for a play if the school ever put one on, but no dramatic readings. They always sounded stupid. About the only thing stupider would be Veronica singing solo.

Robin laughed to herself at the thought of Veronica warbling away. She had an absolutely horrible voice, like those cartoon characters who made dogs yowl when they opened their mouths. Teachers had been telling Veronica to just mouth the words to songs for years.

Then, the way a Christmas tree lights up when a switch is flipped, Robin had a brilliant idea. What if Veronica tried out for the talent show—if she got right up on the stage and sang a song? She had said she'd do anything to get back in Robin's good graces. Would she be willing to make a fool of herself in front of the whole sixth grade?

Robin decided to find out. Now that the weather was growing colder, most of the kids stayed inside during lunch period. All through her tuna fish sandwich, Robin watched Veronica, making sure she stayed put. She could hardly wait to spring her ultimatum on her.

Sharon, chewing slowly, couldn't help but notice Robin's excitement. On Sunday, Robin had told her all that had transpired, so she knew Robin was thinking up an ultimatum. Sharon followed Robin's gaze. "So Veronica and Candy are sitting alone," she observed.

"Veronica may be sitting by herself—if my plan works out."

"You've come up with something. What?" Sharon demanded. Robin explained what she had in mind.

"Wow, that's really mean," Sharon said, dropping her sandwich.

"It's not too mean," Robin said irritably. "Not after what she did to me."

"It sure would humiliate her—if she sings as bad as you say."

"You have to hear it to believe it." Robin laughed.

"Well, there she is." Sharon jerked her thumb toward the big garbage drum, where Veronica was disposing of her lunch. "But I'd think about it if I were you."

"Uh-uh. I'm going to tell her right now."
Robin shoved her leftovers into her lunch sack
and hurried over. "Veronica, I want to talk to
you," she said, tapping the retreating girl on
the shoulder.

"Sure," Veronica said, turning toward
Robin. She looked a little scared.

Robin drew her off to the side, away from
the kids who were pushing and laughing in the
aisles. "You want to make up, right?"

Veronica nodded silently.

"And have the AKGs get back together."

"Yes," Veronica said, her voice low.

"All right. Here's what you have to do. Try
out for the talent show. Sing a song."

Veronica's eyes grew large and her mouth
formed a little O, but no sound came out.

"Say something, Veronica."

"I can't try out," she sputtered.

"Why not?" Robin asked coolly.

"You know how awful I sound when I sing."

"That's the point," Robin responded with
satisfaction. "You'll look about as silly—oh, as
Gretchen trying to do a cartwheel."

Veronica had the good grace to look slightly
ashamed.

"And that reminds me. You also have to
apologize to Gretchen."

Now Veronica found her tongue. "And what

are you going to do if I meet all your demands?"

"I'll make up with you. And I'll consider going back to the AKGs." Robin knew she wouldn't, but she couldn't say so or Veronica would never agree to sing. Putting it this way seemed not quite a lie.

Veronica stayed silent for a few seconds. "Will you talk to the other girls and see if they'll make up, too?" she asked quietly.

"Sure," Robin said expansively. "They'll listen to me."

Veronica thought it over. When she finally answered, she didn't look happy. "Okay, I'll do it."

Robin could barely hear her. "You will?"

"Yes. I'll go to tell Mrs. Volini I'm trying out right now." With that, Veronica turned and stalked away.

Robin watched her receding figure for a few moments. Somehow she didn't feel quite as good as she thought she would.

By the time Robin arrived home, she was tired—tired of thinking about Veronica, tired of thinking, period. She just wanted to slip into her bed and maybe read until dinner, but sounds coming from the basement of heavy objects being pushed and pulled prompted her to see what her mother was up to.

Robin carefully picked her way down the worn wooden steps, wishing her father had replaced the burned-out light bulb as he was always promising to do. There was no way their lower level would ever be confused with a rec room. The unfinished room, with its concrete walls and aging washer and dryer huddled together in the corner, was definitely a basement.

Mrs. Miller, her back toward Robin, was bent over several stacked boxes. She took a book out of one and flung it on the floor. It fell with a heavy thud.

"What are you doing, Mom?"

Her mother gave a little start and straightened up. "Robin, I didn't hear you come in. I'm sorting some of our old books for the library sale."

Robin flopped down on the aged couch that once sat in the living room. "Don't tell me we're actually getting rid of books for a change."

"Even I know when I've run out of space. Besides, I've been carting some of these around since your dad and I lived in our first apartment, and I've never even unpacked them. I'm keeping a few—a very few—and I'm going to let someone else have a crack at them."

Robin reached down and picked up an over-size volume with a tired leather cover and faded gold binding. "The *J* volume of a 1968 encyclopedia? That should get a good price." Robin laughed.

Mrs. Miller looked embarrassed. "I just can't bear to throw books out." She took the volume from Robin and placed it in a large pile. "Books are like people. Each one has a story to tell."

"Books are better than people. They're not mean and obnoxious," Robin said emphatically.

Mrs. Miller observed Robin keenly. "Veronica again?"

Robin picked at the torn fabric of the couch. "I don't know why she has to be so bossy. Plenty of times she was just fun and great to be around."

"You're right," Mrs. Miller agreed. "Veronica does have some excellent qualities."

Robin looked up, surprised. "I can't believe you'd say that."

"The girl has problems," Mrs. Miller said quietly. "She has a great capacity for hurting people, but she also has a pretty magnetic personality. I admit even I was taken in by her for a long time."

"You were, weren't you? I mean, I remember when I used to think you liked Veronica better than me."

Mrs. Miller sat down on one of the large sealed boxes. "I remember that, too. You kept accusing me of wanting Veronica for a daughter."

"That was a long time ago."

"You were in the fourth grade, I think," Mrs. Miller replied. "That's when her parents were going through the divorce and she was over here constantly."

"Before Helen."

"Yes. I think Mrs. Volner thought I was her housekeeper there for a while. But Veronica was always so polite, so grateful for whatever attention I gave her."

"And you were always nice to her," Robin interjected, still a little jealous. "You never really stopped being nice to her, even when you didn't like her anymore."

"She needed kindness, Robin. I tried to remember that, even after I found out how cruelly she could wield her power."

Power. Robin tasted the word. "Veronica sure had a lot of that." Robin was about to tell her mother she was the one with the power now, but Mrs. Miller interrupted.

"Power can be a very dangerous thing. If you have it, it's got to be used wisely. For good, I mean. There's an old saying, 'Power corrupts.' "

Robin made a face. "What does that mean?"

Mrs. Miller thought for a second. "I guess it means that power can destroy. It can destroy things, or it can destroy the person who's using it—if he or she isn't careful."

"But power makes you important," Robin argued.

"True." Her mother shrugged. "But being important can be good or bad. It all depends what you do with your importance. Hey," she said with a smile, "this is a very serious conversation we're having all of a sudden."

"Yeah." Robin forced a laugh. It wasn't making her very comfortable either. Casually, she sat up on the couch. "I think I'll make myself some hot chocolate."

"Robin," her mother asked, eyeing her, "is there anything else you want to talk about?"

Robin shook her head. As far as she was concerned, they had talked too much already. By the time she finished spraying a mountain of whipped cream in her hot chocolate, Robin had decided to just forget the disturbing conversation with her mother. She had the power for once and she was going to use it. Maybe what she was planning for Veronica wasn't very nice, Robin acknowledged, but she deserved it. That's just the way things were.

Robin dressed very carefully the next day. After Veronica got up on that stage and sang like a frog, Robin was going to make sure everyone knew that she was responsible. She might even insist that Veronica tell all of the kids. Then they'd know who was the boss. Robin hummed a little tune as she pulled on a white turtleneck and then a blue Shetland sweater, her initials monogrammed on it, surrounded by small flowers.

As soon as Robin got off the bus, Veronica came up to her, shooing Candy away. She hadn't dressed very specially for her singing debut. She was in her oldest jeans and a sad-looking sweatshirt. Robin couldn't remember when she had ever seen Veronica looking quite like that.

"I did it," she said flatly. "Mr. Jackson knows I'm trying out."

Robin tried to think of something to say. "It's good he's new to Kennedy. Otherwise he'd know you can't sing."

"Yeah, it's great," Veronica said and walked away.

Robin looked around the schoolyard for Sharon. When she found her, Sharon seemed distant, barely answering when Robin told her Veronica was singing as planned.

"You don't seem very excited," Robin said in a hurt tone.

"Why should I be? It's not going to be much fun to watch."

"You're crazy. It's going to be terrific."

"It wasn't that much fun to watch everyone being mean to you."

All day long Robin kept sneaking looks at Veronica. Mostly, she kept her eyes down, looking at her hands. It reminded Robin of something, but she couldn't remember what. Then, as the time for the talent show audition approached, it hit her. Veronica looked just the way Gretchen did, right before she got up in front of the gym class.

Robin felt her resolve weakening. Maybe Veronica deserved to be punished. But with a sudden certainty, Robin knew she couldn't be the one responsible for her humiliation. Oh, part of her still wanted to revel in Veronica looking ridiculous, but Robin remembered too clearly how it felt to be the object of everyone's laughter. Nobody should feel like that. Not even Veronica.

With a sigh, Robin tore a piece of paper from her notebook and began writing: "I changed my mind, Veronica. Forget about singing. Just apologize to Gretchen and we'll be even." She held the note in her hand for a long time. Then she folded it and tossed it to Bobby, who read the name on the outside and slipped it to Veronica.

Robin watched Veronica open the note. It took her a very long time to read, even though it was so short. Finally she looked over at Robin and nodded.

"All right, everyone, let's line up for the tryouts," Mrs. Volini announced. The class noisily put away their books and got to their feet. Robin stood near the door, fiddling with a piece of chalk on the ledge of the blackboard.

"Why did you change your mind?" Veronica's voice said in her ear.

Robin shrugged, not looking at her. "I couldn't be that mean." She turned and faced Veronica. "It would have been pure meanness."

Veronica looked confused. Briefly, she stood there as if hoping for more, but when Robin said nothing, she drifted away. It didn't really matter, Robin supposed. Veronica would just have to figure it out for herself.

When they walked into the auditorium, Mr. Jacobs's sixth grade class was already waiting. "Can we sit anywhere?" Robin called to Mrs. Volini, who was at the end of the line.

"I don't see why not."

Robin looked around the hall until she saw

Sharon waving to her. Bumping people's knees as she cut through a row, she made her way to the seat Sharon was saving.

"Is Veronica going to sing?" Sharon asked her.

Robin shook her head. "I told her she didn't have to."

"You mean you actually let her off the hook?"

"Except for apologizing to Gretchen. If she bothers."

Sharon gave a low whistle. "I can't believe you changed your mind."

"Believe me, it wasn't easy," Robin said ruefully.

"I'll bet."

Robin smiled at Sharon, who smiled back.

As the piano accompanist began running a few scales, Robin turned, almost out of habit, to see where Veronica was sitting. She was off in the corner, locked deep in conversation with Gretchen Hubbard.

ILENE COOPER has been a children's librarian and a consultant for ABC Afterschool Specials. Currently she is a book reviewer for a major publication. Ms. Cooper has written for network television and is the author of *Susan B. Anthony,* a biography for children, and *The Winning of Miss Lynn Ryan,* which is also about students in Kennedy Middle School.

Ms. Cooper is married to Robert Seid, a television director. They live in Highland Park, Illinois.